CLUB TIMES
For Members' Eyes Only

Like father, like son...

I put my foot in it this time, members, but I'm going to plead Temporary Hardware Store Stupidity. Okay, so Hawk Wainwright and I smashed into each other when we were both examining screws and washers (no, I didn't do it on purpose). Can you blame me for getting riled when he growled at me? As if I should do ballet while picking out a washer or a screw! I said, "You are just as crabby as your father." His death glare catapulted me into another stratosphere and I left the hardware store empty-handed. Oops.

To cheer myself up, I went over to Mrs. McKenzie's dress shop, because if you stand near the fitting rooms, you can hear the latest water-cooler dirt from the cream of Mission Creek society. Kate Wainwright and Rose Wainwright-Carson whispered about the fact that

interior designer Jenny Taylor has a *past*. (Those quiet ones are always hiding something.) And poor Jenny has Hawk Wainwright as her next-door neighbor. I have to warn her never to borrow a cup of sugar from him!

But here at the Lone Star Country Club, we embrace all—the loud ones (you know who you are), the quiet, the brave, the spineless and even the scary ones of Mission Creek. We are a family.

So bring it on at the Lone Star Country Club. The sooner, the better!

About the Author

SHERI WHITEFEATHER

lives in Southern California and enjoys ethnic dining, summer powwows and visiting art galleries and vintage clothing stores near the beach. Since her one true passion is writing, she is thrilled to be part of the LONE STAR COUNTRY CLUB series, where she had the pleasure of learning about a wondrous place called East Texas.

Sheri is married to a Muscogee Creek silversmith. They have a son, a daughter and a trio of cats— domestic and wild. She loves to hear from readers. You may write to her at: P.O. Box 17146, Anaheim, California 92817.

SHERI WHITEFEATHER

LONE WOLF

Published by Silhouette Books

America's Publisher of Contemporary Romance

Special thanks and acknowledgment are given
to Sheri WhiteFeather for her contribution
to the LONE STAR COUNTRY CLUB series.

 SILHOUETTE BOOKS

ISBN 0-373-61361-X

LONE WOLF

Printed in U.S.A.

Welcome to the

LONE STAR COUNTRY CLUB
EST. 1923

*Where Texas society reigns supreme—
and appearances are everything.*

*Could a Native American rebel uncover the secrets
hidden in his neighbor's hardened heart?*

Hawk Wainwright: An outsider his entire life, Hawk
was drawn to his mysterious neighbor whose quiet
beauty was impossible to ignore. But this lone wolf
would need to overcome his own past before he
could plan a future with Jenny.

Jenny Taylor: After an abusive marriage forced her
to run away and start a new life, Jenny vowed she'd
never fall for someone based simply on looks and
lust. Now, though, an outsider seemingly with no
hidden agenda has made Jenny feel passion once
again...stirring her soul like no man ever has.

The Mercados of Mission Creek: One of the
most powerful families in Mission Creek has taken
a special interest in the kidnapping of baby Lena. Is
it possible that patriarch Johnny Mercado is involved
in the abduction?

THE FAMILIES

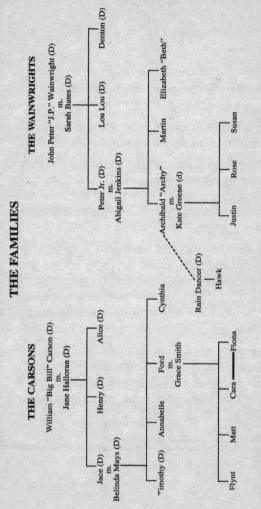

THE CARSONS

William "Big Bill" Carson (D)
m.
Jane Halloran (D)

Jace (D)
m.
Belinda Mays (D)

Henry (D)   Alice (D)

"Timothy (D)   Annabelle   Ford   Cynthia
                             m.
                             Grace Smith

Flynt   Matt   Cara   Fiona

THE WAINWRIGHTS

John Peter "J.P." Wainwright (D)
m.
Sarah Bates (D)

Peter Jr. (D)   Lou Lou (D)   Denton (D)
m.
Abigail Jenkins (D)

Archibald "Archy"   Martin   Elizabeth "Beth"
m.
Kate Greene (d)

Justin   Rose   Susan

Rain Dancer (D)

Hawk

D   Deceased
d   Divorced
m.   Married
- - -   Affair
———   Twins

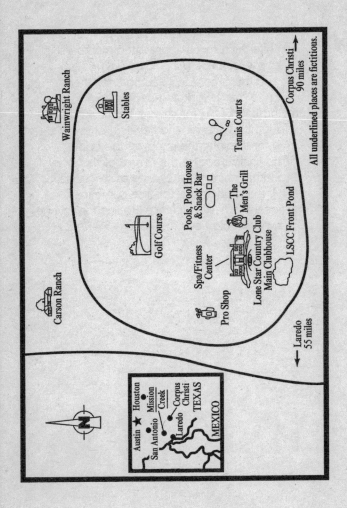

Wainwright Ranch

Carson Ranch

Stables

Golf Course

Pools, Pool House
& Snack Bar

Spa/Fitness
Center

The
Men's Grill

Tennis Courts

Pro Shop

Lone Star Country Club
Main Clubhouse

LSCC Front Pond

← Laredo
55 miles

Corpus Christi
90 miles →

All underlined places are fictitious.

Austin ★ • Houston

San Antonio • Mission
Creek

• Corpus Christi

• Laredo

TEXAS

MEXICO

N

To Margaret Marbury
for offering a much-appreciated membership
to the LONE STAR COUNTRY CLUB.
To the other LSCC authors for their
hard work and dedication.
To my husband, Dru, for sharing the hawks in his life.
To Kimberly Payne and her dog, Cheyenne,
for inspiring the puppy in this book.
And finally, because the nature of this story
is too important to categorize as strictly fiction,
I'm including the toll-free number of
National Domestic Violence Hotline for anyone
who should need it: 1-(800) 799-SAFE.

One

Hawk Wainwright walked out onto his front porch, then stopped when he saw her.

The pretty woman next door.

She knelt on the grass, planting flowers in her yard. Curious, he watched her.

A soft breeze blew her hair across her face, shielding a delicate profile. She wore old jeans and a simple cotton blouse, but she managed to look ethereal. He suspected her eyes were blue, rivaling the color of the sky.

But the angelic beauty seemed determined to keep to herself. She never spoke to him, never met his gaze or acknowledged him in any way.

Not that Hawk expected special treatment. He wasn't the friendliest person in the neighborhood. Nor were folks drawn to him. Since his youth, Hawk had been considered an outcast. Then again, he didn't give a damn about socializing in Mission Creek. This town hadn't been particularly kind to him, even if it had been home for as long as he could remember. He lived on the outskirts of Mission Creek, and for good reason.

Hawk was the unwanted, illegitimate son of one of the richest men in the county. And being the Wainwright bastard had taught him how to live on the fringes of society, how to thumb his nose at his daddy and his half siblings. They meant nothing to Hawk. Nothing at all.

Nothing but a childhood ache he'd long since outgrown. Standing six foot one with a set of broad shoulders and a pair of dark, unforgiving eyes, he was no longer a kid hoping his prominent, white daddy would notice him.

Thirty-three-year-old Hawk Wainwright was an Apache, a man who trained horses, rescued injured raptors and asked Ysun, the Creator of the Universe, the Apache Life Giver, to guide him.

And who was the pretty lady next door? he wondered, as he started down the porch steps to retrieve his mail. And why was she so shy? So cautious?

Maybe she'd heard the gossip about him. Eight years ago, Hawk had dated a pampered, rich, breathtakingly beautiful white girl. But after they'd slept together, he'd discovered that she had no intention of introducing him to her family or bringing him into her social circle. She had, however, treated him like a prized Indian stud, whispering quite naughtily that her roommate wanted a turn with him.

Stunned, Hawk hadn't responded to the lewd offer. But just days later he'd approached both girls at a local bar. After kissing one and then the other, he'd quietly told both of them to go to hell. Naturally those hot, public kisses had culminated in a much-talked-about scandal.

But he'd learned his lesson, and these days Hawk no longer felt the need to explore his Anglo side by dating white women. Instead, he avoided them.

He glanced at his neighbor again. She was as fair-skinned as they came, but she still fascinated him. He couldn't help but admire the way her gold-streaked hair caught the light or the way a spray of geraniums bloomed like a rainbow at her feet.

Let it go, he told himself. Stay away from her.

He turned and opened his mailbox, then sifted through the envelopes until an unfamiliar name printed on one of them caught his eye.

Jennifer Taylor.

He checked the address and saw that it was incorrect. The letter, bearing the logo of a fashion magazine, belonged to the lady next door.

Shooting his gaze in her direction again, Hawk weighed his options. Should he just put the letter in her mailbox? Or use this as an excuse to satisfy his curiosity and talk to her?

Curiosity won, along with a self-admonishing curse. He was doing a hell of a job of avoiding her.

Stuffing his own mail in his back pocket, he headed toward her, cutting across the adjoining driveways that separated their houses.

"Jennifer?" he said when he reached her.

She started at the sound of his voice, which told him she had been unaware of his presence.

Still kneeling on the ground, she looked up at him, shielding her eyes with a gloved hand.

"Are you Jennifer?" he asked.

"Jenny," she said a little too softly. "I'm Jenny."

"I think this belongs to you."

She removed her gloves and stood. But when she reached out to take the envelope, she teetered.

"Are you all right?" he asked. She couldn't seem to catch her breath, and the sun flushed her skin, making it look hot and pink.

"Yes," she said, but her flushed face went pale.

Too pale, he thought.

The envelope fell from her hand, fluttering to the ground. And in the next instant, she was going down, too. Passing out, Hawk realized.

He reacted quickly, even though he had never been in the company of a fainting female before. Reaching forward, he caught her, and she sagged against him like a rag doll.

Unsure of what else to do, he lifted her into his arms and then stood beneath the blinding sun, like an Apache renegade who'd just scared the wits out of an innocent, young captive.

Now he knew why he avoided white women, he mused, mocking his penchant for trouble. He only wanted to meet his new neighbor, not create another scandal.

Hawk adjusted Jenny, cradling her against his chest. She didn't weigh much, but handling her felt awkward just the same.

He made his porch steps in record time. Turning the doorknob, he shouldered his way inside. Next he deposited her on his cedar-framed sofa, her clothes twisting a little as he did.

Hawk stepped back to study her, hoping she would rouse on her own.

But she didn't. Jenny remained motionless, her crumpled cotton blouse exposing an intriguing slice of skin just above the waistband of earth-smudged jeans. He couldn't help but notice her navel. Or the lean, yet feminine curves of her body.

Hawk frowned. Now he really felt like a renegade, checking out an unconscious woman.

Then quit looking, he told himself. And figure out a way to revive her.

Like what? Mouth to mouth?

Oh, yeah. That's the gentlemanly thing to do, he thought as he rummaged through his kitchen for the first-aid kit he kept on a cluttered shelf.

Hawk grabbed the plastic box, opened it and found what he was hoping to—smelling salts.

Returning to Jenny, he knelt before her, broke the packet and waved it beneath her nose.

She stirred instantly, jerking as she regained consciousness. When their eyes met, he noticed how blue they were. And how wary.

Jenny pulled back, trying to put some distance between herself and the man staring at her. He was much too close, his face just inches from hers. She could see the tiny lines around his eyes, the pores in that rich, copper skin, the small scar near his mouth that gave his frown an element of danger.

His hair fell in an inky-black line, but light spilling in from the window sent a sapphire sheen over each shoulder-length strand.

Around his neck, a turquoise nugget dangled from a leather thong. Both ears were adorned with small black claws—talons as sharp as his cheekbones.

She knew he was her neighbor, but she'd done her best to avoid him.

"You passed out," he said.

Jenny merely nodded, unable to find her voice. His, she noticed, was as rough as the Texas terrain.

Did she fall into his arms? she wondered, mortified at the thought. All she remembered was the world turning a hazy shade of white.

He sat on the edge of the coffee table. "Has this ever happened before?"

"No," she lied. She'd fainted once when she was pregnant, but that wasn't the reason she'd lost consciousness this time. There was no way she could be pregnant. Jenny hadn't been with anyone since her divorce.

"I'm sorry I troubled you," she said. "But I'm okay now." She shifted to a sitting position to prove her point, but the movement lacked conviction. She was still a bit dizzy, her mouth as dry as dust.

He frowned at her, the scar twisting into that menacing shape again. "You don't look okay to me." He rose to his full height. He stood tall and powerfully built, broad of shoulder and narrow of hip. His clothes consisted of a white T-shirt, dark jeans and a pair of knee-high moccasins.

Clearly, no one would mistake him for anything other than what he was—a tough, striking, modern-day warrior.

"Sit still," he ordered. "I'll get you a glass of water."

Although she wanted to escape, to rush home and recline on her own couch, she did as she was told. In spite of her neighbor's gruff demeanor, he seemed genuinely concerned. But Jenny still feared upsetting him. Men, she knew, weren't always what they seemed.

And this one, with his commanding voice and scarred frown, was probably used to getting his way.

He returned with a glass of ice water and resumed his seat on the edge of the coffee table.

Jenny wanted to tell him that he didn't have to sit so close, but she couldn't summon the courage to be that bold. Or that rude, she supposed. He was only trying to help.

"Sip slowly," he said.

"Thank you." The water tasted clean and refreshing. Revitalizing. "I just got over the flu. And I was tired of being cooped up in the house."

"So you went outside and worked in the sun?"

"I enjoy planting flowers," she responded, hoping it wasn't a dumb thing to say. Roy used to tell her that she often made dumb, girlish comments.

She tried not to think about her ex-husband and what he would do if he saw her with this man. But Roy was always on her mind, and she was always worried about him being nearby, stalking her the way he'd done back home in Salt Lake City.

"Planting flowers is fine, I suppose. But now it appears you've got a touch of sunstroke. No wonder you passed out."

He shook his head and sent those black talons dancing. Jenny watched them spin, thinking how primitive they made him look.

They lapsed into silence, so she took another sip of water and glanced around his house. The layout was just like hers, she realized, but the decor, with its sturdy furnishings, was undeniably masculine. An oak gun case filled with lever-action rifles made a strong, noticeable statement.

She scanned the rifles, recognizing what appeared to be an original Winchester Yellow Boy, the legendary 1866 model. Western relics had become a significant part of her design business, and she spent most of her free time scouting and researching special pieces.

"By the way, I'm Hawk," he said, drawing her attention back to him.

"Hawk." She repeated the name. Somehow it fit. She could see him gliding through the air. Or swooping down to prey on a smaller, weaker animal.

Like an unsuspecting female? she asked herself with a familiar shudder.

She bit her lip. "I should go. I've taken enough of your time already."

"Not yet."

He reached out and put his hand on her cheek, and she froze, stunned and speechless. His hand was cool and big, his palm rough and callused.

"I think you have a fever." He moved to her forehead, brushing her bangs aside.

Jenny held her breath, resisting the urge to push him away, to protect herself from the emotion he inflicted. The affectionate gesture brought back too many memories.

But she couldn't tell him that. Not without admitting that Roy used to stroke her face. And then raise his fists when his temper flared.

Hawk removed his hand. "I'll get you a couple aspirin."

"No. I just need to go home and rest." She rose to leave, handing him the water.

He walked her to the door, then set the glass on a nearby table. "I forgot about the letter you dropped."

"I'll get it." She glanced outside, assuming it was still on the grass somewhere.

"Why don't you let me find it? I can slip it in your mailbox. You should stay out of the sun. Maybe take a tepid bath to break the fever."

"All right," she managed, and Hawk smiled. It gentled his rawboned features, softening the scar and adding a flicker of light to those dark eyes.

"Bye, Jenny."

"Bye." She turned away quickly, knowing he

watched as she cut across the lawn and headed to her own house.

Taking a deep breath, she stared straight ahead, refusing to glance back or wave or smile. Jenny Taylor knew better than to get too friendly with a young, powerful, good-looking man.

Four days later Jenny wheeled her shopping cart out of the market, her grocery bags filled with frozen entrées, canned goods and fresh salad fixings. Cooking traditional meals for herself was too much trouble, so she prepared quick, simple things. Occasionally she dined out, enjoying the Yellow Rose Café at the Lone Star Country Club. She wasn't a member of the club, but she was the interior designer who'd landed the prestigious job of designing the decor of the new wing. And although that job was complete, she'd since been hired to redecorate some of the original guest rooms. The Lone Star Country Club was an icon in Mission Creek, a Western resort catering to the crème de la crème of Texas.

"Hey, lady," a youthful voice called out. "Do you want to adopt a puppy?"

Jenny turned, realizing she was the lady being singled out for the adoption.

Two adolescent boys, brothers, from the looks of them, sat in a shady spot in front of the market, a cardboard box between them.

A small, yippy bark echoed from the box, drawing Jenny closer.

"He's a real nice dog," the older of the two boys said. "And he's the last one. We already gave the rest of the litter away."

Unable to help herself, she peered into the box. The

tan-and-black puppy yipped again, then wriggled uncontrollably for her attention.

The dog had green eyes, a narrow face and large floppy ears. Its rounded feet looked like four white socks.

She knelt to pet him and was rewarded with a sweet doggie grin. He was adorable, she thought, warm and soft and huggable.

Should she take him home? Give him a cozy place to sleep?

Instantly Jenny drew her hand back and came to her feet. How could she commit to a pet? She didn't know how long she'd be staying in Mission Creek. Or where she would go if Roy found her. In a sense, she lived on the lam, running like a criminal from a nightmarish past.

"Cute critter," a deep voice said from behind her.

Jenny turned to see Hawk, dressed in jeans and a denim shirt, a straw Stetson dipped over his dark eyes. The beaded hatband and lone feather dangling from it made his ethnic features seem more pronounced. The talons in his ears glinted dangerously in the April light.

Her heart slammed into her throat. Was he following her?

Of course not, she told herself a moment later. He had to come into town to shop, too.

"How are you feeling?" he asked.

"Fine," she responded, wishing her heart would quit dominating her throat.

Avoiding eye contact, she glanced at the ground. And noticed Hawk's feet. He wasn't wearing moccasins today. Instead, he sported a pair of dusty black cowboy boots, the toes turned up, the leather scuffed.

"I just got off work," he offered.

"Oh." Was he a cowboy of some sort? A ranch hand perhaps? His clothes were nearly as dusty as his boots.

"I'm a horse trainer," he said, as though he'd just read her mind. "I lease a barn at Jackson Stables."

Neither spoke after that. Jenny tried to relax, but she could feel Hawk's eyes on her.

He stared at her hair, at the gold-streaked tresses that used to be a quiet shade of brown. She touched a strand self-consciously. She wasn't used to being a blonde yet, but she'd changed the color hoping Roy wouldn't recognize her so easily.

Hawk shifted his gaze to the dog. "Are you in the market for a puppy?"

"I don't think I have enough time for him. My career keeps me busy." And her fear of being tracked down by her ex-husband kept her on the move. "He is adorable, though." She gave the floppy-eared mutt a loving glance.

"He looks like he's got some Australian Shepard in him." The boys perked up, realizing they had a potential adoptive parent kneeling to check out the dog.

"He's part beagle, too," the older kid said.

"That's some combination." Hawk picked up the puppy, then stood and faced Jenny. The young dog wiggled excitedly in his arms.

"I've never seen a mixed blood quite like this one, have you?"

She shook her head, distracted by Hawk's choice of words. The dog was a mixed *breed*. Mixed *blood* was a term more suited to humans.

And then suddenly she knew why he'd made that

subconscious error. Hawk was of mixed blood. She hadn't noticed the Caucasian in him before, but she could see touches of his white ancestry now. His skin was more copper than brown, and the long, slim line of his nose bore a shape she often associated with English aristocracy. Of course, on Hawk's strong-boned face, it didn't look quite so genteel.

Jenny had never given her own ancestry much thought, but she suspected Hawk's mattered to him. Or at least the Native American side did.

"Will you dog-sit once in a while?"

She blinked. "I'm sorry. What?"

"The puppy. I'm thinking about keeping him."

She gazed at the dog and laughed when he nudged her with his paw. He looked snug as a bug in Hawk's sturdy arms. Fluffy and sweet. Now she wanted to go back into the market and buy him a cart full of chewy treats and squeaky toys.

"Yes," she said, without thinking clearly. "I'll dog-sit as often as I can."

"Great." Hawk's lips curved into that fleeting smile, the one that gentled his features and softened the scar near his mouth.

Jenny only stared. And then her heart went crazy, pounding like an out-of-control drum.

Dear God. How could this be happening? She was attracted to Hawk. After all she had been through with Roy, and now this. She wasn't ready to feel this way, to confront a physical attraction.

"I have to go," she said abruptly.

"Are you sure you can't stay for a few more minutes?" He held up the puppy, and the floppy-eared little guy yipped happily at her.

"No," she responded a bit nervously. "I can't."

Hawk watched Jenny wheel her cart across the parking lot. Why was she so cautious? Why did she run away from him every chance she got?

At this point, he didn't think his reputation had preceded him. Whatever plagued Jenny went much deeper than frivolous gossip.

There were moments she reminded him of a wounded creature—a skittish filly or a bird with a broken wing.

Of course, Hawk had experience in both those areas. But he'd never gotten close to a woman with a fragile spirit.

Then again, he'd never gotten close to anyone.

"Are you gonna keep the dog, mister?"

He glanced at the kids. "Yeah, I am. Is that okay with you two?"

"Sure. He needs a home."

Well, he's got one now, Hawk thought, as the puppy continued to wiggle like a furry, wet-nosed worm. Reaching into his pocket, he removed his wallet and handed the boys some cash.

Dumbfounded, they stared at him. "He doesn't cost anything. We're giving him away."

"I know, but I don't mind paying for him." Hawk wanted the dog to know that he was just as valuable as a pedigreed dog with papers. Animals, like humans, he believed, sensed their worth.

"Our dad said he was the runt."

"Right now maybe. But look at the size of these feet." He held out one of the pup's big clumsy paws. "He's not going to be a runt forever."

The boys grinned and accepted the donation just as Hawk's cell phone rang.

He walked away for some privacy. "Hello?"

"Hawk, it's Tom Jackson. I think you better get back to the barn."

"Why? What's wrong?"

"You've got a client waiting on you. And he's the impatient sort."

Hawk frowned. He wasn't expecting anyone at the barn, not at this hour. "Then put him on the phone."

The other man paused. "I'm sorry, but I'd rather not. I think you need to handle this in person."

"All right." Whoever the client was, he certainly had the owner of Jackson Stables jumping through hoops. "I'll be there as soon as I can."

Hawk loaded the puppy into his truck and decided not to speculate about who was waiting for him. If someone had a professional beef with him, he would find out what the problem was and remedy it. Hawk considered himself an ethical man, a man who didn't brawl over things a firm handshake and a calm, rational attitude could fix.

The commotion next to him caught his attention. The dog wouldn't sit still. The feisty little critter paced the bench seat, finally settling on Hawk's lap with an insecure whine.

"It's okay." He scratched the puppy's head. "You can stay there for now. But sooner or later, you'll have to toughen up."

By the time Hawk reached Jackson Stables, the dog was asleep. He chuckled and turned into the driveway that led to his barn.

And then he spotted the truck and horse trailer bearing the Wainwright logo.

What the hell was this?

Hawk parked his rig, exited it and set the puppy on the ground.

Squaring his shoulders, he went around to the back of the trailer where he saw none other than Archy Wainwright—the son of a bitch who'd spawned him—leaning against it.

Two

Primed for battle, Hawk forgot all about being calm and rational. "What the hell are you doing here?"

Archy made a slow turn, meeting Hawk's gaze. He stood tall and well built, a man fit and trim for his age. "I brought you some business."

"Really?" Hawk's voice oozed with sarcasm, his blood running cold. "Now, why would you do that?"

"To see if you're any good."

Pride, pure and primitive, gushed through his veins. "Of course I am. I'm an Apache. We've always been better horsemen than your kind."

Archy lifted a bushy brow, his clear blue eyes sparkling with challenge. A custom-made cowboy hat rested casually on his head, and his skin was tanned and weathered. Hawk refused to see himself in the other man, even if their height and the breadth of their shoulders were the same.

"My kind?" Archy asked finally.

"Rich, useless Texans."

The wealthy rancher gestured to the trailer, his tone tight and tough. "If that's how you feel, then accept the work I'm offering. Prove how good you are, Apache."

"I don't have to prove a damn thing to you." Nor did he want his father's tainted money. "You're nothing to me." Nothing but the womanizer who'd taken advantage of Hawk's mother and then refused to acknowledge Hawk as his son. "I'd rather do business with the devil."

"Well, as it happens, you're not bearing Lucifer's name. It's mine you're using, and I have the right to know if you can break a horse the Wainwright way."

"I don't do anything the Wainwright way," Hawk said, keeping his voice steady and his fists clenched. "And the only reason I'm using your name is because my mother wanted me to. Now get the hell away from me, old man. And don't ever come back."

"You're a cocky bastard, I'll say that much for you." Archy turned his back on Hawk and headed for his truck.

Yeah, I'm a bastard, Hawk thought. But I was once a little boy, an innocent kid who wanted his daddy to care.

The puppy barked at the Wainwright rig, giving Archy a piece of his mind. Of course, the older man was already behind the wheel, his door closed, his windows secure, but the show of loyalty made Hawk feel good just the same. The dog's youthful voice had lowered an octave, the hairs on his back rising.

Hawk's hackles were up, too. He'd run into his dad off and on throughout the years, chance meetings neither had orchestrated. But Archy had never come gunning for his son. He'd never looked Hawk straight in the eye and challenged him to prove that he deserved the Wainwright name.

And his doing it today made Hawk hate him even more.

Once Archy's truck and trailer disappeared down the road, he picked up the pup.

"Let's go home." Hawk needed to unwind, to

jump in the shower and allow the water to pummel his body. "And then I'm downing a few beers to take the edge off," he told the dog. "And fixing both of us something good to eat." He wasn't about to let Archy twist his stomach into a knot and destroy his appetite.

Twenty minutes later Hawk pulled into his driveway, killed the engine and cursed. He'd just remembered that he hadn't returned to the market. His fridge was empty.

Damn it. He didn't have the energy to drive back into town. He couldn't deal with a public place, all the noise and people.

He wanted to be alone, wanted to shower, drink a few beers, grill a thick, juicy porterhouse and reward the dog with table scraps for barking aggressively at Archy.

But now it seemed Archy had won.

Weary, Hawk leaned against the seat and caught movement through the passenger window.

It was Jenny, he noticed, watering her plants. He sat quietly, just watching her, letting her image soothe his soul. She looked so pretty, so angelic, her floral-printed dress billowing in the breeze.

The puppy stood on his hind legs, determined to check out the view. Hawk smiled. Even the dog wanted to see her.

And then the image spoiled.

Mrs. Pritchett, the snoop from across the street, was heading straight for Jenny.

The older woman glared at Hawk's truck, telling him all he needed to know. She'd seen him pull up, and now she was going to warn Jenny about him.

He knew exactly what she would say. *Watch out*

*for that one, dear. He's just like his mama. She se-
duced Archy Wainwright, ruining that poor man's
marriage.*

Hawk closed his eyes. His mother had died a long
time ago, but her name was still being dragged
through the mud.

And Hawk, of course, had created his own scandal,
the kissing escapade Jenny was sure to hear about.

Jenny felt someone nearby. She turned and saw a
gray-haired woman making determined strides to
reach her.

Sensing trouble, she adjusted the hose nozzle, shut-
ting off the water. The lady wore an old-fashioned
housecoat and a pair of white sneakers, her face
pinched in a superior expression. She wasn't collect-
ing for a charity or selling door-to-door cosmetics.
This busy bee had "nosy neighbor" written all over
her.

"I'm Mrs. Pritchett from across the way." She
pointed to a prim yellow house. "And I've been worried about you. The way that man watches you."

Jenny's heart slammed against her rib cage. Did
this have something to do with Roy? Had this lady
see him lurking about? "What man?"

"Why, that Indian, of course."

Jenny's heartbeat stabilized. Roy wasn't the man
in question. "You mean Hawk?"

"Who else would I mean? I saw what he did last
week. He carted you right into his house."

"I wasn't feeling well that day," she explained,
defending her neighbor. "I'd spent too much time in
the sun, and I fainted. Hawk was kind enough to
help me."

Mrs. Pritchett motioned to his driveway. "He's sitting in his truck, watching us right now. Or watching you, I should say." She pointed a bony finger, a gesture not unlike the one the Wicked Witch of the West used on Dorothy. "I'd stay away from him if I were you. He isn't the type a pretty, young thing like yourself should trust."

Jenny glanced quickly at Hawk's truck, catching a glimpse of him behind the wheel. "He was a perfect gentleman," she countered, even though his rugged good looks and dark, penetrating eyes made her much too aware of being female.

"How would you know? You were unconscious." The other woman cleared her throat. "Do you know who he is? Who his parents are?"

No, Jenny thought, but you're just dying to tell me.

"His mother is dead now, but she went by the name Rain Dancer. She was tall and slim, with hair down to her rear."

Was long hair a sin? Jenny wondered.

"Well, Rain Dancer set her sights on a married man. A rich, prominent rancher, no less. And being the way men are, he couldn't resist her. Slut that she was."

Jenny flinched. She hadn't expected Mrs. Pritchett to be quite that cruel. "So this wealthy rancher is Hawk's father?"

"That's right. Archy Wainwright. Surely you've heard of him."

Stunned, Jenny widened her eyes. She hadn't just heard of him, she was indebted to him. The Wainwrights were founding members of the Lone Star County Club, and it was Archy who'd recommended her to Joe Turner, the architect overseeing the renovations at the club.

Mrs. Pritchett moved closer, delighted by Jenny's reaction. "Hawk isn't a legitimate member of the Wainwrights, even though he uses their name. They don't recognize him as one of their own. But who can blame them? That half-breed is trash, just like his mother. Why, a while back he actually kissed two white girls in a bar, one right after the other. Spicy kisses, if you know what I mean. Then he walked out of the place without uttering a word." Mrs. Pritchett moved closer still. "It was quite a scandal, considering those young ladies were high-society types." She snorted. "No one knows why he provoked a scene like that. But I've heard several theories. Some say—"

A vehicle door slammed.

Jenny and Mrs. Pritchett turned simultaneously.

Hawk had exited his truck and now trapped Jenny's gaze from across the yard. He knew, she thought. He knew exactly what Mrs. Pritchett had been saying.

"Oh, my." The older woman took a step back. "He's coming this way. Why, the nerve."

Yes, he was coming their way—all male and all muscle, the puppy from the market at his heels.

"Hello, ladies," he said. "Jenny. Mrs. Snitchett."

"*Prit*chett," the old woman corrected, glaring at him with her wicked-witch sneer.

"Of course." One corner of his mouth twitched in the semblance of a smile. "Mrs. Bitchett."

The old lady huffed. "I don't have to stand here and take this."

"Then don't," Hawk said.

Mrs. Pritchett pointed her finger at him. "I warned

her about you." She turned to Jenny, her finger still raised. "Don't say I didn't warn you."

With that, she stalked across the yard, holier and mightier than thou.

Hawk and Jenny stared at each other. Suddenly neither of them knew what to say. She chewed her bottom lip and he stood like a statue, the feather on his hat lifting in the breeze.

"She's a malicious old woman," Hawk said finally.

"She certainly doesn't like you."

"No, she doesn't." He paused, then blew out a breath. "But I would appreciate it if you reserved judgment and formed your own opinion of me. You know, instead of letting the gossip sway you."

Jenny nodded. "I think that's only fair."

"Thanks."

He sent her one of those fleeting smiles, and she felt an uncomfortable stir of attraction. Did he really kiss those two girls?

"I guess I should let you finish watering." Hawk glanced at the flower beds. "Oh, no. I'm so sorry."

Jenny turned and saw why he was apologizing. His new pet had uprooted every last one of Jenny's geraniums and was grinning at both of them like a mischievous hyena. And to top it off, the dog was covered in mud.

"You little scoundrel." Hawk grabbed the pup by the scruff of the neck, the way a scolding mother dog would do. "I'll buy you another batch of flowers, Jenny."

He gave the dog an exasperated glance, and the little scoundrel swished his tail, spraying his master with mud.

Hawk cursed, and Jenny stifled a giggle. A second later they both burst out laughing.

"Will you help me hose him off?" Hawk asked when their laughter faded. He still held the dog by the scruff, but the pup squirmed something fierce.

"Sure." She turned on the water and decided she liked Hawk Wainwright. But then, she liked his father, too. She stole a glance at Mrs. Pritchett's house, certain the old woman watched from her window.

Was it true that the Wainwrights didn't acknowledge Hawk? It did seem odd that he lived in a modest home, while Archy and his family resided on a sprawling ranch.

"Can you adjust the water level?" he asked.

"Oh, of course." Jenny turned the flow to a mild spray, and between the two of them, they got the puppy clean.

Hawk still had flecks of mud on his jeans, but she noticed he was smiling.

Jenny smiled back at him, and the moment turned soft and gentle. The puppy rolled in the grass, kicking up his feet and exposing his belly.

"Will you have dinner with me?" Hawk asked.

Jenny's breath lodged in her throat. Was he asking her on a date? A quiet meal, companionable conversation, a good-night kiss?

She couldn't do it. She couldn't—

"I'll order a pizza, and we can sit on my porch," he suggested.

Her breath returned, and she pulled oxygen into her lungs. Pizza on his porch. That sounded safe enough.

"All right," she heard herself say.

He smiled again, and she wished his smile wasn't so charming. Roy's smile had been charming, too.

He'd been her white knight, the man who'd swept her off her feet. And then dragged her into a dungeon of pain.

"What do you want on it?"

Still lost in thought, she gave him a blank look.

"The pizza," he clarified. "What toppings would you prefer?"

Suddenly she couldn't focus on something as simple as pizza. Not with the dungeon lurking in her mind, the dank, cold reality of knowing Roy was out there somewhere. How often did she wake up screaming? Or hug her knees to her chest and cry?

"It doesn't matter," she said. "Order whatever you want."

"Of course it matters. You must have a preference."

Did she? She used to eat what Roy told her eat, dress in the clothes he told her to wear, be the wife he wanted her to be.

"Pineapple," she told Hawk. Roy hated pineapple on pizza. "And Canadian bacon." Her ex-husband detested that, too.

"You got it. Now I better hop in the shower. I'll come by and get you when the food arrives."

He picked up the puppy, and Jenny watched him walk back to his house. The dog peered over his shoulder, and she smiled, feeling a spark of freedom, a shimmer of independence.

But when she went inside to bathe and put on some clean clothes, she panicked. Roy would kill her if he knew she was having dinner with another man.

Not figuratively kill her. He would actually put his hands around her throat and squeeze the life out of her.

But Roy wasn't here, she reminded herself. And they were divorced. She had every right to share a pizza with her neighbor.

Her tall, gorgeous neighbor. The man who made her heart beat much too fast.

Hawk told himself he wasn't nervous. He wasn't a schoolboy with a foolish crush. He was a grown man who'd quit dating ages ago.

Hawk had occasional sex of course. Quiet, discreet affairs with women from his own race, women who accepted the lone wolf in him. But he didn't date. And he especially didn't court blue-eyed, color-treated blondes.

Like Tanya.

He'd been on the verge of falling in love with Tanya, of losing his heart and soul. But he was just a game to her. She'd only wanted him because he was dark and forbidden, the Indian stud, the back-street lover who was supposed to service her. And her roommate.

He picked up the pizza, balancing two cans of soda on top of the box. Jenny wasn't anything like Tanya. Blue eyes and bleached hair didn't make them the same.

Hawk headed for the door and felt something nudge his boot. He looked down and saw the pup, eager to go with him.

"I don't think so, pal."

The puppy whined, and Hawk felt like a heel. "All right. But behave yourself. We've got a lady to impress."

The dog grinned, and Hawk narrowed his eyes. Was he being conned?

"I'm not sure I can trust you."

He received an innocent bark in return, a sound that translated to *I'll be good. I promise.*

"You better mean that."

Another gentle bark. *I do.*

"You won't take off running once you get a lick of freedom?"

"Woof," the dog said again, his green eyes big and beguiling. *No, sir. Not me.*

Hawk opened the door, and the ball of fur flew past him. He cursed and nearly dropped the pizza.

Chasing the damned dog wasn't possible, so he placed the food and drinks on a small table on his porch and strode across the lawn to Jenny's house.

The puppy was already waiting on her doorstep, where he'd left muddy footprints. He wasn't covered in the stuff, but he'd obviously taken a detour through the flower beds to reach his final destination.

"Don't you dare grin at me," Hawk warned.

The dog sniffed a fern, instead.

Jenny's porch was cozier than Hawk's. She'd decorated it with a gathering of potted plants. A swing that had been there for years creaked in the breeze.

He knocked and waited for her to answer.

She appeared in a white blouse and jeans, her gold-streaked hair fastened in a ponytail. The ribbon-enhanced style made her look sweet and girlish.

And it made Hawk feel as if he was fifteen again, too tall for his age, with sweaty palms and boyish desire that heated his loins.

"The pizza is here," he said.

"Okay." She knelt to pet the dog and laughed when she spotted his dirty feet. "He can't keep those socks clean, can he?"

Hawk was still stuck on how pretty she looked, on how mouthwateringly good she smelled. He detected the faint aroma of raspberries, dipped in just a hint of custard. Or whipped cream. Or just plain feminine skin.

"You smell like dessert."

She looked up at him, her voice suddenly shy. "It's one of those body mists. I bought it at the market today."

"I like it."

She smiled, barely meeting his gaze. "Thank you."

They walked side by side to his house, the puppy dancing around them.

He offered her one of the cedar chairs and handed her a soda and a slice of pizza, then realized he should have brought a couple of plates outside, not to mention a napkin or two.

Well, hell. He probably seemed uncivilized, like the barbarian most people thought he was. "I'll be right back." He left and returned with the plates and napkins.

Jenny accepted both gratefully. He sat in the chair opposite hers and went after two slices of pizza. He was starving, his stomach grumbling at the mere sight of food. He took a hearty bite and frowned at the dog. The little scoundrel was begging.

He tore a corner of the crust and handed it over. He'd already scrambled the puppy the last two eggs in the fridge, but now the pooch wanted pizza, too.

"I'm buying some dog food tomorrow," he said. "And I'm going to train this guy to behave." Hawk looked at Jenny. "I'm good with animals."

She watched the dog hit him up for another bite. "Yes, I can see that you are."

"They don't usually take advantage of me. In fact, they never do."

"Which one of us are you trying to convince?" she asked. "Me or him?"

"You." Hawk smiled at her. "He already thinks he can con me." He shifted his gaze to the dog. "But you're in for a rude awakening, you mangy mutt. Enjoy your last few hours of freedom, because in the morning, you're headed for boot camp."

The dog yawned, and Jenny laughed. "Have you thought of a name for him yet?"

"No." Hawk opened his soda and took a swig. It felt good to be near Jenny, to look into her eyes and see a glimmer of friendship brewing. "I'll probably name him the Apache way."

"What do you mean?" she asked.

"I'll give him a temporary name until he earns another one."

"I think he's already earned a name."

She pointed to the dog's feet, and Hawk grinned.

"Muddy," they said in unison, laughing like a couple of kids who'd just shared a private joke.

But all too soon, their laughter faded. They sat across from each other, their gazes locked, the sun setting in the sky like a rebellious streak of fire.

Heat crackled between them, the kind of energy that stilled the air.

She twisted the napkin on her lap, and he felt like a dumbfounded fifteen-year-old all over again.

"I think Muddy is a perfect name," he said, grasping for something to say.

"So do I." She latched on to his words like a lifeline, glancing at the dog for a diversion. "It fits him."

"Yeah." He told himself to keep the conversation

going, to not let the heat come back. Not now, while they were still stumbling into a newfound friendship.

"Do you want to come to the South Texas Raptor House with me sometime?" he asked.

She made a puzzled expression. "What's a raptor?"

"A bird of prey, like eagles, owls, falcons and hawks. I volunteer at a center that's dedicated to rehabilitating injured raptors and releasing them back into the wild. Of course they have some permanent residents, too. Amputees and other birds that can't survive in the wild."

She studied him as though analyzing his association with the center. "Did you earn your name, Hawk?"

"Yeah, I did. But I was just a boy at the time. I came across a Cooper's hawk that had been hit by a car. I wanted to scoop it up in my jacket and take it home, but somehow I knew better. I sensed that I wasn't qualified to handle it."

"So what did you do?"

"I ran home and told my mom, and she contacted the Raptor House. They cared for it until it was well enough to be released." He smiled at the memory. "I felt like I'd done something really important, like I was part of that hawk's survival, part of its spirit. My mom called me Hawk after that."

"And you learned to work with raptors when you were old enough?"

"That's about the size of it." He took another swig of his soda. He was glad she hadn't questioned him about his birth name. He didn't want to admit that he'd been named Anthony Archibald Wainwright after his father. Of course Jenny probably didn't know anything about Archy, other than what Mrs. Pritchett might have told her. Jenny didn't run in the same social circle as the Wainwrights, of that much Hawk was certain.

"So, are you interested in a tour of the center?" he asked.

She nodded. "Yes, but I have a busy week coming up."

"There's no rush." Sooner or later he would get to know Jenny Taylor, who she really was and why she seemed so secretive.

Three

The Lone Star Country Club spanned two thousand acres of prime Texas land. The main clubhouse, a four-story pink granite building, had French windows that overlooked the rolling lawn of the award-winning eighteen-hole golf course. Six tennis courts and three swimming pools provided the members with athletic entertainment. The Empire Room, the Men's Grill and the Yellow Rose Café prepared meals to suit every occasion.

Jenny entered the Yellow Rose Café, where a hostess greeted her.

"May I sit in Daisy's section?" she asked.

"Certainly." The hostess smiled and led her to a table that offered an enchanting view of the patio.

Jenny liked the sunny decor. Yellow-gingham tablecloths added a touch of spring, as did the planter ablaze with marigolds, petunias and snapdragons. The planter separated the café from a small, bustling bar, making a pretty yet practical statement. Everything about the country club fascinated her, and she was grateful for the opportunity to continue her association with it. Her work was the one source of pride in her life, the foundation for her sanity.

She glanced at the menu and decided on some light fare. She'd just completed a meeting with the painting contractor, but she had other meetings after lunch. This wasn't a leisurely day.

"Hello, Jenny."

Daisy arrived at the table, pen and pad in hand. The waitress was a stunning bleached blonde, with a dark complexion and a curvaceous athletic build. But in spite of her beauty, Jenny sensed something sad about her. There was pain in her eyes, deep and unsettling, a look Jenny often recognized in the mirror.

Was Daisy Parker running away from her past, too? Hiding the way Jenny was? Keeping secrets that haunted her at night?

Daisy always had a ready smile, but that didn't mean a thing. She still seemed nervous somehow, preoccupied and fearful.

"What can I get you today?" Daisy asked.

"The mixed greens and a glass of raspberry iced tea."

"What kind of dressing?"

"The house will be fine."

Why had Daisy lightened her hair? she wondered. For the same reason she herself did? Or was Daisy just a brunette who wondered if blondes really did have more fun?

Maybe it was silly to worry about Daisy, but Jenny couldn't help it. Deep down, she wanted to befriend the woman, get close to her, ask if she needed help. But how could Jenny aid someone else? Her own emotions were still a mess. She barely had the strength to confront her own fears, let alone tackle Daisy's problems.

The waitress sent Jenny one of those carefully controlled smiles and darted off with her order.

A short time later Jenny's meal arrived. As she ate,

the café bustled around her, members of the country club coming and going.

Just as she finished her salad, she spotted Archy Wainwright across the room heading her way. She reached for her tea and acknowledged his gaze.

Archy was a business associate, someone she respected and admired. But discovering that he was Hawk's father put an odd spin on seeing him.

"Well, hello, Jenny," the older man said when he reached her table. "May I?"

"Yes." She gestured for him to join her and scanned his features with newfound interest, looking for a likeness to Hawk. She couldn't find an overwhelming resemblance, but she had to admit that Hawk had Archy's powerful stature and deep, gruff voice.

"I hear you've been doing an outstanding job," he said. "The board is pleased with your work. And your dedication. You've put in some long hours."

"Thank you. I enjoy what I do. And the overtime keeps me busy."

"Glad to hear it." He gestured to Daisy, and the waitress came right over. "I'd like a cup of coffee, darlin', and bring Jenny a piece of that tasty apple pie."

"Thanks, but—" Jenny tried to protest, but Archy cut her off, giving Daisy more instructions.

"Don't mind her, just bring the pie. And be sure to put everything, including that rabbit food she ate for lunch, on my tab."

Daisy obeyed his command. Within minutes Jenny had a fresh-baked dessert sitting in front of her.

"It's delicious," she said after she'd taken a bite.

"Nothing beats a slice of warm apple pie. Now tell

me, Jenny, have you made some friends in Mission Creek? Working overtime is fine, but socializing is important, too.''

"I..." She stalled to take a much-needed breath. "I had dinner with a neighbor last night." With your son, she added silently.

"That's good. Now the reason I stopped by was to let you know the club is hosting a spring ball, and you'll be receiving an invitation." He lifted his coffee, his eyes on hers. "I can arrange an escort for you, if you'd like. Unless, of course, you've already made the acquaintance of an appropriate young man.''

Momentarily stunned, she stuck her fork into the pie, trying to gather her wits. A spring ball? An appropriate young man?

Like Hawk?

Jenny tried not to panic. No, not like Hawk. She couldn't ask him to a ball his father had invited her to. Nor could she dance with him. She was barely handling the first few stages of friendship.

"This would be good business," Archy said, sensing her apprehension. "You'll rub elbows with all the right people."

People who might hire her for future projects, she realized. Yes, it was good business, but she couldn't do it.

"It's still a month away," he added. "So you've got time to buy a fancy dress and go to the beauty parlor or whatever it is you women do to make men fall at your feet."

She managed a weak smile. "I'm flattered by the invitation, but I'm not much for parties."

Archy shook his head. "You're too pretty to be a wallflower."

And she was too edgy to date. "I'm still getting settled in. New town. New people. I'm just not ready for a ball."

"All right. But if you change your mind, the offer still stands."

The pie hit her stomach like a rock. She had the feeling Archy wasn't going to let this lie. He would continue prompting her for the next few weeks.

Maybe he thought it was his duty to bring her out of her shell, to introduce her to Texas society.

The older man had taken her under his wing since the day she'd arrived on the job, guiding her in a paternal fashion.

And she had been touched by his kindness, by the softness she saw in his eyes.

But things seemed complicated, now that she'd met his illegitimate son.

Jenny worked another long day. When she pulled into her driveway, dusk had fallen.

She sat in her car for a moment, then decided she wouldn't be able to relax until she told Hawk about her association with his father.

Although she wasn't certain that their budding friendship could take the strain, she knew it was the right thing to do.

She'd promised to form her own opinions of Hawk, not judge him on the basis of hearsay, and he owed her a similar courtesy. She'd met Archy before she even knew Hawk existed. She wasn't betraying one for the other.

Jenny knocked on his door, expecting to hear the

puppy bark. But when Hawk answered her summons, wearing nothing but a pair of jeans, she lost her composure.

His hair, long and damp, was combed away from his face, making the sharp talons in his ears stand out even more. His chest, broad and bare, exposed a knee-weakening display of muscle. She didn't dare peek at his stomach.

"Jenny," he said. "You look great."

"Thank you." She smoothed her jacket. She wore a professional beige suit, the skirt riding several inches above her wobbling knees. Her blouse and pumps were beige, as well. The only spot of color was a blue silk scarf. She knew it matched her eyes.

She didn't comment on how he looked. What did one say to a half-naked man?

"Come in." He stepped away from the door, and she entered his house.

She tried to relax, but couldn't quite manage it. She hadn't expected to catch him fresh from the shower.

"Where's Muddy?" she asked.

"Asleep. He tired himself out, chewing half the pillows in the house. I might have to crate him during the day. Or bring him to the barn, I suppose. He'd probably get into less trouble there." Hawk gestured for her to sit. "Do want you a soda? Or a beer or anything?"

"No." She glanced at the couch, but couldn't bring herself to sit. "If this is an inconvenient time, Hawk, I can stop by tomorrow." When his hair wasn't damp. When he wore more clothes. When she could think clearly.

"I wasn't doing anything. You're welcome to stay.

I'm just going to grab a beer. Are you sure you don't want anything?"

"Yes, I'm sure."

She sat primly on the edge of the couch, and he returned with a bottle of Mexican beer.

"Is something wrong?" he asked.

"No." She shook her head, then glanced around the room. He'd given the house a cabin-type feel, with rough woods and animal skins. His moccasins were tossed in a corner, and an end table was littered with old newspapers. Masculine clutter, she supposed, although she didn't have any experience with it. Roy had been fanatical about keeping things tidy.

She spotted a framed photograph on another small table. The little boy in the picture had to be Hawk, the woman holding him, his mother.

Rain Dancer.

The name fit. She was the most exotic-looking woman Jenny had ever seen. One could imagine her dancing in the rain, her jet-black hair glistening beneath the moon.

No wonder she'd bewitched Archy.

She was spellbinding.

Jenny turned to find Hawk watching her. He'd taken a chair near the fireplace. His jaw was set in a tight line, his eyes suddenly more black than brown.

"Did Mrs. Pritchett say something about me again?" he asked. "Or about my mother?"

"No. I haven't seen Mrs. Pritchett. But I spoke to your father today. Archy Wainwright is a business associate of mine."

Hawk didn't move, not one muscle. He didn't even blink. "A business associate?"

"Yes." Jenny folded her hands on her lap. Suddenly the room seemed smaller, the walls more compact. She wished there was a window open, a shift of air. "I'm an interior designer. I came to Mission Creek to work with the architect on the renovation of the new wing at the Lone Star Country Club. And now that it's complete, I'm redecorating some of the original guest rooms."

"And what do you think of good old Archy?" he asked, one corner of his mouth lifting in a cynical smile.

"I like him," she answered honestly. "He's been very kind to me. I landed the Lone Star Country Club contract because of him. He recommended me to the architect."

Hawk took a swig of his beer, but his eyes were still dark and unyielding. "How did Archy become familiar with your work?"

"I was the designer on a chain of steak houses in Utah. Archy is affiliated with the owner." She continued to keep her hands clasped on her lap. "I won an award for that project. For the authenticity and creativity of the Old West theme."

"Have you told him I'm your neighbor?"

"No." She felt as though she was being interrogated for a crime. "I didn't feel it was my place. I don't know anything about your relationship with your father, Hawk."

"I don't have a relationship with him. He's never acknowledged me as his son. Surely Mrs. Pritchett told you that much."

"Yes, but if you want to tell me your side of the story, I'm more than willing to listen."

"What's the point?" He pulled on the beer again. "It won't change your mind about Archy."

At a standstill, they stared at each other.

Jenny took a ragged breath and made the first move. ''You're the first person I've met in a long time that I thought I could be friends with. I'm not very social, and…'' She paused to study his hardened features, stopping herself before she told him too much, before she admitted that she wasn't allowed to have friends in the past, that her acquaintances consisted of Roy's peer group.

''I don't see how we can be friends,'' Hawk said. ''Not with the way you feel about Archy.''

She stood, the wobbly feeling coming back to her knees. ''I know. But I can't make myself dislike him.'' The opportunity Archy had given her to come to Texas had changed her life. It had allowed her the chance to escape, to start over somewhere new.

Because Hawk remained silent, she walked to the door. ''I should go home now. I'm tired and hungry.'' And hurting. She hadn't realized how important Hawk had become until this moment.

Their blossoming friendship had given her a glimmer of hope, a belief that they shared something unique. That she could spend more carefree evenings eating pizza and chatting with a man who wasn't asking more from her than she was capable of giving.

But now he wanted her to choose sides, to pick him over his father.

It was an unfair demand and one she refused to be forced to make.

Jenny raised her chin and left Hawk's house, determined to prove her point.

But as soon as she reached her front door, the fa-

miliar threat of tears stung the back of her eyes, reminding her of how lonely and isolated she really
was.

Hawk hadn't seen Jenny for nearly a week. And
now he stood by the bed of his truck on a quiet Sunday morning, wondering what to do with the flat of
flowers he'd purchased for her.

He'd gotten them to replace the geraniums Muddy
had torn from the ground, but he didn't know whether
to leave them on Jenny's porch or just go ahead and
plant the damn things.

Hawk glanced at the dog. Muddy was loose on the
lawn, playing in the grass, staying out of trouble for
once.

He lifted the cardboard flat, deciding he'd leave
them on Jenny's porch. Why deprive her of the joy
of arranging them? She liked planting flowers, and he
would probably bungle the job, anyway. He didn't
mind mowing the lawn or pulling weeds, but deco-
rative gardening eluded him.

Hawk carried the load with ease—until he reached
Jenny's steps, where he nearly stumbled.

She sat on the porch, occupying the swing, pretty
as a spring picture. A simple white cotton dress
draped her ankles, and her hair was loose and just a
little bit messy.

He set the flowers near the rail.

"You didn't have to do that," she said.

"I told you I would replace them."

Their eyes met, and for instant, he imagined touching her hair. A wild strand blew across her face, as
rebellious as the South Texas wind.

He could smell the enticing aroma of citrus groves

stirring in the air. Or was the fresh scent coming from Jenny?

Hawk wanted to tell her that he missed her, but he couldn't bring himself to say something like that. They barely knew each other. He had no business missing her.

He frowned and she glanced away. She looked so damn vulnerable, so lost.

Like a dove with damaged wings.

"I'm sorry," he said.

Her gaze shot back to his. "For what?"

"For being an ass." Why did women always make men explain themselves? Why wasn't "I'm sorry" ever taken at face value? "For getting ticked off about your business association with Archy."

"You're not angry because he recommended me for a job. You're angry because I like him."

Hawk frowned again. He couldn't stand the thought of Archy influencing her life. It just gave him one more reason to hate the man.

Frustrated, he fantasized about kicking the porch rail and splintering the wood, but he held his temper. He wouldn't let Archy rule his emotions.

"We should spend more time together, Jenny."

Her eyes grew wide. "We should?"

"Yeah. If you're still willing, I want to be friends."

"I'm still willing."

"Good." When he sat beside her, the swing creaked. She smiled shyly at him, and he inhaled her fragrance.

"It *is* you," he said.

"What's me?"

"The lemons I smell."

"It's another one of those body mists," she responded, rocking the swing a little, her voice as shy as her smile. "I bought the variety pack."

Suddenly Hawk got a craving for lemon meringue pie. Well, hell, he thought, maybe he wanted more than friendship. Maybe he wanted to explore the man-woman thing happening between them and see how good it felt to kiss her.

Silent, they both watched Muddy toss a new toy around Jenny's yard. At some point the dog had followed Hawk onto her property.

"He plays fetch," Hawk said. "But he's not consistent. Sometimes he'd rather eat the ball."

She laughed, but the silence that followed became awkward. That man-woman thing was creeping in, and he sensed it made Jenny uncomfortable.

She was attracted to him, but she didn't want to be, at least not in a physical sense, he thought. But why?

"So you're originally from Utah?" he asked, realizing he knew little about her.

"Yes. Salt Lake City."

"Do you still have family there?" he asked.

"No."

"How old are you?"

"Thirty. How old are you?"

"Thirty-three," he responded, realizing getting Jenny to talk about herself wasn't easy.

Well, one of them had to open up, he thought. "Do you still want to hear my side of the story?" he asked.

She turned to face him. "You mean about Archy and you and your mother?"

He nodded.

"Yes, I'd like that very much. I saw your mother's picture. She was very beautiful."

So are you, he wanted to say, still itching to touch her hair, to brush her bangs out of her eyes.

To kiss her.

When she blinked those stunning blue eyes, he cleared his throat.

"My mom worked at the Lone Star Country Club. That's how she met Archy. She was a riding instructor. Of course, Archy didn't need to learn to ride, but he was around the stables quite a bit." Hawk paused, then explained further. "The Wainwrights and the Carsons used to own the horses at the club. And I suppose they still do. Have you met the Carsons?"

"Most of them. They're the other family who established the club. I've heard there's a feud between the Carsons and the Wainwrights."

"Yeah, it's been going on since 1927 or so." And Hawk had been tempted to join the feud, to ally himself with the Carsons, to work on their ranch just to spite Archy. But he'd stayed away from both wealthy families. "Anyway, Archy and my mom had an affair. She knew he was married, but she'd been young and naive, just impressionable enough to believe he would leave his wife. Of course, he never had any intention of ending his marriage. When my mom told him she was pregnant, he refused to acknowledge that the child she carried was his."

"What did Rain Dancer do?"

For a second Hawk only stared. He wasn't aware that Jenny knew his mother's name. "She left town and went to live with my grandmother in Oklahoma. We're Chiricahua Apache. Most of the Chiricahua live on a reservation in New Mexico, but there is still a small number residing in the vicinity of Apache, Oklahoma."

"So were you raised in Oklahoma? Did you come back to Mission Creek on your own?"

"No. My grandmother died when I was five, and Mom decided to return to Texas to introduce me to my father, to make another attempt to get Archy to acknowledge me."

"She could have filed a paternity suit."

"Yeah, she could have. But she was too proud to do that. Besides, this wasn't about money. It was about honor. And love."

Jenny smoothed a strand of her hair. She watched Hawk with a gentle expression, with compassion in her eyes. "Do you remember meeting Archy for the first time?"

"Yeah." Hawk recalled it vividly. "He looked at me for the longest time. And for a moment I thought he was going to smile or ask me a question. Or shake my hand. But instead, he turned to my mom and said, 'He's not mine. Anyone can see that he's not mine.'"

"I'm sorry," she said.

Hawk blew out a tight breath. "When Archy walked away, my mother said, 'He knows you're his, and someday he'll come forward and give you his heart.' I wanted so badly to believe that."

Muddy leaped up the porch steps and skidded onto the wood. Jenny leaned down to pick him up. As she resumed her seat, his dirty feet made marks on her clean white dress.

Content to be in her arms, the pup quit squirming and calmed down, settling into her lap. Hawk envied him the luxury, the warmth, the soft feminine touch.

"I can't believe Archy did that to you," she said, continuing their conversation. "He seems kinder than that."

"I guess that's what my mom thought, too." But Archy had that effect on women, a charm they couldn't seem to resist. Hawk knew better. "The one bright spot was that Archy's wife left him when she found out about me. He didn't get away with being a liar and a cheat. Of course, he blamed me for the destruction of his marriage, and so did his other children. Walking around with the Wainwright name isn't easy, but I won't give it up. My mom wanted me to have that name. In her eyes, it legitimized my birth."

For a moment he thought about Archy's recent challenge regarding his name. There was no point in mentioning that to Jenny, he supposed. He didn't intend to hear from his dad again. "The Wainwrights are rich and powerful, so that makes people curious about me, too. But I've learned to deal with the gossip, with people like Mrs. Pritchett."

Jenny stroked the dog. "Mrs. Pritchett said some awful things about you and your mother. The next time I see her, I'm going to tell her that she has no business spreading vicious rumors."

"Thanks, but she won't listen. She's already formed an opinion of you now, too." And that meant Jenny would become part of his world. "Being my friend isn't going to be easy," he said. "People will wonder about you. They might even make up stories about us. They'll think I'm corrupting you."

"I know," she responded quietly.

Yes, he thought, she knew. But knowing might not be enough. If their relationship stirred up too much gossip, Jenny's reputation could suffer.

Hawk hoped and prayed that he was worth the risk.

Four

A week later Jenny spent the morning at the Lone Star Country Club stables, wandering around the facility, hoping to feel some sort of connection to Hawk's deceased mother. It seemed like an odd thing to do, but Jenny couldn't help herself. She was curious about Rain Dancer, curious about the woman who'd given birth to Archy Wainwright's illegitimate son.

Caught up in the moment, Jenny studied the breezeway barn, the fenced arena and the paths leading to South Texas riding trails. Spring bloomed in the air, carrying the scent of hay, horses and flowers.

Money bloomed in the air, too. The aura of wealth.

And Jenny stood in the center of it all, wondering about a woman who had worked there thirty-four years ago.

She couldn't condone Rain Dancer's affair with a married man, but she could picture her, young and naive, caught up in a world not her own.

Had she been in love with Archy? Had he simply swept her off her feet?

Maybe it had been the other way around. Maybe Rain Dancer had knocked Archy off his feet. Maybe the beautiful Apache had been everything his wife wasn't.

Archy's wife could have been staid and cold—the

overly proper, calculating socialite. Then again, she could have been kind and loyal, someone her husband had treated like a doormat.

Either way, Archy Wainwright was becoming less and less of a hero in Jenny's eyes. What he'd done to Hawk proved that he—

"Are you planning on riding today?" a masculine voice asked from behind her.

Jarred from her thoughts, Jenny turned to face the intruder.

"Archy?" For a moment she wondered if he was a figment of her imagination, an unwelcome apparition she'd conjured out of thin air.

He stood tall and broad, his gaze fixed steadily on her. The brim of his hat shaded his face, but his eyes crinkled warmly at the corners.

He looked fatherly somehow. Big and protective.

He moved closer, and she cursed her emotions. She wanted to hate him, to blame him for hurting Hawk, yet somehow she knew the older man cared about her.

It made no sense. How could he treat her like a daughter and turn his back on his son?

"I'm not riding today," Jenny said finally. "I'm just touring the stables." Searching for a connection to Rain Dancer, she added silently. Trying to satisfy her curiosity about Archy's clandestine lover.

Was it a coincidence or a strange twist of fate that he'd shown up this morning?

"Have you toured the barn?" he asked.

"No, not yet."

"Then allow me to be your guide. I'm familiar with the stock."

He placed his hand on her shoulder. His touch was firm yet gentle. She thought about Hawk's mother and

Archy's scorned wife, wondering if they had
screamed and clawed at each other the way wounded
women often did.

Jenny couldn't imagine fighting over a man, but
she knew how it felt to have someone break her heart.

"Are you all right?" he asked.

"Just a little preoccupied." What would he say if
she told him what was on her mind?

He gave her shoulder a paternal squeeze and led
her to the barn, alive with sights and sounds. Grooms
went about their daily routines, and horses whinnied,
as if chatting with their equine neighbors.

Archy gestured to a flashy bay. "If you decide to
ride, I recommend a Wainwright mount."

"As opposed to a Carson mount?" Jenny asked,
knowing he was teasing about the notorious feud.

He laughed. "Why, of course." His laughter faded,
and he made a serious face. "Did you know that the
Wainwrights and the Carsons have an heir? My oldest
daughter married one of the Carson boys, and they
just had a baby."

Which, Jenny assumed, added even more fuel to
the feud. Archy's eyes held plenty of emotion.

"Congratulations," she said, realizing Hawk was
an uncle, as well. The Wainwrights might not accept
him, but he was still their blood.

He grunted. "My new grandson is a fine boy, but
I don't know how in hell I'm supposed to share him
with Ford Carson."

"Very carefully," she suggested, thinking about
the baby she'd lost.

He turned to look at her. "You're a nice girl,
Jenny. Too nice, I suspect."

She frowned at him. "What does that mean?"

"It means I'm worried about you." He shifted his stance, his boots scuffing the ground. "Have you heard the rumors, the things people are starting to say? It's a bunch of crap, I'm sure, but that doesn't mean being talked about hurts any less."

Because her palms turned clammy, she rubbed them on her jeans. "What rumors?"

"They say you're having some wild, crazy affair." Archy's brow furrowed. "I don't think it's necessary to mention your alleged partner's name. We both know who he is. And we both know he has a seedy reputation. He could ruin a nice girl like you."

"He's a good person," Jenny defended. "He's my friend." And this conversation was making her uncomfortable. Needing a breath of fresh air, she headed for the door, passing a row of box stalls on her way out.

Archy followed, and they stood beneath the vast Texas sky, a warm breeze stirring between them.

"You have no right to warn me about him," she said.

"So the gossip doesn't bother you?"

"Of course it bothers me." It made her stomach roil; she didn't want to be the subject of lewd speculation. "But I'm not doing anything wrong. And Hawk," she added, using the name Archy was avoiding, "isn't taking advantage of me."

The older man held up his hand. "Then I'll back off. But I swear to you, little lady, if he hurts you, I'll come gunning for him."

Jenny didn't respond, but apparently Archy didn't expect her to. He walked away without another word, which told her she was trapped between the father and the son, between two men who hated each other.

* * *

Hawk checked his watch, wondering if Jenny would come outside tonight. Meeting on his porch while Muddy played on the lawn had become their neighborly routine.

And now he was worried that she wouldn't show.

Muddy raced around the grass, darting in and out of the shrubs. He still wasn't the most well-behaved critter, but he had a personality that made him more human than dog.

The pup barked, and Hawk came to his feet. That was Muddy's "Hi, Mom" greeting, which meant Jenny had decided to join them, after all.

Hawk crossed the lawn, then stopped when he saw her.

Her hair was pinned up in a messy style, her feet were bare, and her dress caught the rays of the setting sun. She looked at one with the elements, like a rose blooming right before his eyes. For an instant Hawk thought he could see her spirit, the beauty that lived inside her.

And then the image was gone, burned away by the frown in her eyes.

He moved closer. "Evening, Jenny."

"Hawk." She sighed, and he knew her distress involved him.

"What's wrong?" he asked.

"I saw Archy at the club today. It was a personal meeting."

He tried to subdue the blast of anger. "Personal?"

She nodded. "I vouched for your character. I told him what a good person you are."

"You did?" Stunned, he could only stare.

"Yes. He found out that we know each other, and

he warned me to be careful around you. But he did it in a concerned way, more out of respect for me than a grudge against you." She paused, visibly uncomfortable. "It was so awkward. I feel as if I'm caught in the middle somehow."

Hawk felt exactly the same way. He didn't like Jenny being put in a position where she felt she had to defend him, especially to that son of a bitch Archy. But more importantly, her support pleased him. For the first time in his life, someone had stood up for him. Someone gave a damn.

"Thank you," he said.

She nodded, but she didn't smile. "There's more, Hawk."

He braced himself for another blow. His life, it seemed, was full of them. Hard knocks. Fists to the gut.

"There's a rumor going around that we're lovers. Mrs. Pritchett probably started it, but apparently it's circulating all over town."

He hadn't braced himself well enough. This unexpected blow hit him straight in the groin. It was, he decided, a blend of discomfort and arousal, something he'd never experienced before.

He didn't want the folks of Mission Creek gossiping about him and Jenny. He didn't want his life to taint hers. But on the other hand, imagining himself as her lover had an appeal he couldn't deny.

"They've got us sleeping together already? Jeez, I've never even been in your house."

"I've been in yours."

True, but she hadn't been anywhere near his bed. Or near his body. He met her gaze, wishing she found a little humor in this. Something, anything to ease the tension. And the tightness beneath his zipper.

"I'm sorry, Jenny."

"It isn't your fault."

Maybe not, but his arousal made him feel guilty as hell. "I think we should have a talk. I should probably tell you about my past. You know, since you're stuck with the stigma of being my supposed lover."

She twisted a strand of her hair. Stray locks spilled from the topknot pinned haphazardly on her head, giving her a tousled, just-out-of-bed quality.

"Are you going to tell me about those two girls?"

He nodded.

"Did you actually kiss both of them?"

"Yes."

Her cheeks colored, and he figured her face would be flaming like a flamingo by the time he got to the sex part.

"Maybe we should go inside," he said. "I'd rather not have this conversation out here."

"Should we go to your house or mine?" she asked, chewing her lip in that nervous little way of hers.

"That's up to you."

She chose hers, so he walked beside her, Muddy nipping at their heels.

Jenny's house brimmed with femininity—lace curtains and ruffled pillows, ornate woods and a collection of miniature carousel horses that brought a touch of wonder to his heart. Everything looked delicate, yet magical. Like her.

Muddy made himself at home, curling up in a cozy corner for a nap, but Hawk stood in the center of the living room, feeling sorely out of place.

"How about some iced tea?"

She darted into the kitchen before he could say yes or no, then returned with two tall glasses.

He accepted one, sat in a cream-colored chair and caught a whiff of her fruit-inspired body mist. He wondered if her lingerie drawer was spiced with those fragrant little sachet bags, or if her nightstand held crystal bowls filled with dried flower petals or potpourri or whatever it was called.

His dresser, he knew, made a typically male statement, as it was the place he routinely dumped his keys and wallet. And nothing spiced his underwear drawer. Nothing but a box of lubricated condoms.

Jenny sat on the sofa and waited for him to begin. He tasted the tea. It was cold, but a little too sweet.

"There was a time when I wanted to be the kind of guy who would fit into a place like the Lone Star Country Club," he said. "I guess it had to do with being Archy's kid." And with foolishly hoping that his high-society family would accept him. "It didn't matter so much when my mom was alive, but after she was gone, I started analyzing my life, who I was and where I came from."

"How old were you when your mother died?" Jenny asked.

"Eighteen." He looked up from the tea. The glass was sweating in his hands. "She was killed in a car accident just a few months after I graduated from high school."

"Oh, Hawk, you were just a boy."

The tenderness in Jenny's voice made him uncomfortable. He wasn't looking for sympathy. "I mourned her the Apache way. I destroyed her belongings, and I cut my hair. I cried, but I didn't sing. The Chiricahua have no death songs." And the memory still haunted him, the sound of the owl hooting on the night she died.

He gazed at Jenny. He could see that he was making her emotional. He sensed her mother was gone, too. "It's not good to talk about death. It's not something the Chiricahua normally do," he added, letting her know why he was changing the subject.

"I understand," she said.

They sat quietly for a moment, and he imagined touching her, holding her close and breathing in her scent. Jenny was special, he thought. She had the spirit of a dove.

"About eight years ago," he began at last, "there was a girl who was really important to me. Her name was Tanya, and she was white. Blond and blue-eyed, like you."

Jenny twisted a strand of her hair. "Was she one of the girls you kissed?"

He nodded. He hadn't told anyone this story, and he wasn't quite sure how to tell it now. "Tanya and I weren't from the same social circle. She was a country-club girl—rich and beautiful and spoiled. But she seemed vulnerable, too. Her family controlled everything she did, or at least that was the impression she gave me."

"How did you meet her?"

"She bought a horse from me, and we started dating soon after that. But it was a secret relationship. Her family wouldn't have approved of her seeing someone like me." Hawk set his iced tea on a nearby table. "It was a whirlwind romance, I suppose. Exciting, fast. At the time she was everything I wanted. We felt so right together." And he felt strange talking about this, baring his soul to Jenny about the woman who'd destroyed him. "I wasn't in love with her, but I was damn close. I could feel it happening, and it scared me. I never imagined needing someone so badly."

He looked at Jenny and wondered if she'd ever felt that need, that desperation for another human being. He didn't know much about her, and he could see that she wasn't going to offer further information. She just sat, watching him with those captivating blue eyes. He hoped to God he didn't start feeling desperate for her, that she didn't climb inside him the way Tanya had. Hawk never wanted to be on the verge of losing his soul again.

"I thought that I was important to Tanya, that eventually she would tell her family about me," he said. And he'd fooled himself into believing that his Wainwright name would make a difference. "I was looking for acceptance, I suppose. Tanya was the first, in fact the only, white girl I've ever dated."

Jenny's blue eyes locked on to his. "She hurt you, didn't she."

For one long, uncomfortable moment, he wanted to shift his gaze, but then he caught the cloud of pain in Jenny's eyes. And suddenly he knew that someone had done something far worse to her than what had been done to him. The look on her face was much too raw, he thought. Much too wounded.

"Yeah," he said. "Tanya hurt me." But who hurt *you?* he wanted to ask Jenny.

She studied him silently, waiting for him to continue, and he wished the rest of his story wasn't so damned sordid. "Tanya and I became lovers. We couldn't get enough of each other. Sometimes she would even call me in the middle of the night. You know, hungry for me.''

Jenny blinked, and he exhaled a rough breath. Her cheeks were growing pink, and her shy blush made him feel a bit too warm. On the verge of an unwelcome arousal, he reached for the discarded tea and wet his mouth. There was no way to tell this tale without mentioning the sex.

''I had no idea that Tanya was thriving on the secrecy, on the whole forbidden aspect of our relationship.'' He gulped the tea and felt a tiny ice chip slide down his throat. ''Not until she told me that her roommate wanted to sleep with me.''

Jenny's mouth formed a shocked ''Oh,'' and for a second, they just stared at each other.

''Tanya was actually willing to let me service her roommate,'' he said, breaking the uncomfortable silence. ''Like I was some sort of prized stud.''

The blush on her cheeks deepened. ''What did you do?''

''Nothing, not at first, anyway.'' He drank the rest of his tea. ''I suppose Tanya thought her naughty suggestion would turn me on,'' he said. ''I am a guy, and her roommate was pretty hot. Some men fantasize about stuff like that.'' He paused, cursing his honesty. ''But I was half in love with Tanya, and the whole thing made me feel sick and dirty.''

''Then why did you go into that bar and kiss them?'' she asked. ''They *are* the two girls you kissed, aren't they?''

''Yeah, but I hadn't meant to do that. It wasn't intentional. It just sort of happened.''

She gave him a disbelieving look, and he wondered how to explain a man's emotions to a woman.

"Kisses don't just happen, Hawk."

Oh, yes, they do, he thought. If there was a chance in hell he could get away with it, he would kiss Jenny right now. She was chewing her bottom lip, sucking it between her teeth, making him thirsty again.

"I went to that bar because it was the last place they were expecting to see me. It was their turf, an uppity nightclub for the country-club crowd. When they saw me, they pretended I was a stranger. But I knew damn well that if I went to their condo later, they'd sleep with me." And that had infuriated him. "So I decided to challenge them in public. I asked Tanya to dance, but she refused. And then I asked her roommate, and she refused, too."

"I don't see how that led to kissing," Jenny said.

"I was standing really close to the roommate. And I thought, she won't dance with me in public, but she'll go to bed with me. This girl I barely know. It seemed so damn twisted. So what I did was twisted, too. I grabbed her and kissed her. And then I turned to Tanya and did the same thing. Afterward, I told them both to go to hell." He gave Jenny a humorless smile. "It created this big scandal. Not just for me, but for them, too."

"So you got your revenge."

He shrugged. "In a way, I suppose I did. But some of the rumors that started to circulate were pretty ugly, and I realized then that it had been a stupid thing to do." He looked up from his empty glass. "Stories about me trying to lure Tanya and her roommate into an orgy surfaced first. But when that got old, people started speculating in another direction. They said that I'd purposely shown disrespect for two high-society women to make some sort of racial statement. You know, the half-breed bastard, intent on desecrating the white community.''

Muddy woke up from his nap and nudged Jenny's knee. She petted him, and Hawk noticed how soft and feminine her hands were, with her clear nails and slim, delicate fingers.

"I wasn't trying to show disrespect for anyone," he went on. "My pride was bruised, so I reacted. I lashed out.''

She glanced up from the dog. "It was more than your pride, Hawk. It was your heart.''

"I guess.'' Embarrassed, he shrugged. "I've been over Tanya a long time. And I've kept my affairs discreet ever since. I don't try to call attention to myself, but no matter what I do, people still gossip.''

"You're the illegitimate Wainwright," she said. "I suppose it comes with the territory.''

"Yeah, but now I've dragged you into it, as well.'' And his father, of all people, had warned her to be careful around him. That hurt more than he cared to admit.

She lifted Muddy onto her lap. "I can handle it.''

Could she? he wondered. Could she stand the dirty looks and sneers behind her back? The whispers that she was foolish enough to let the Wainwright half-breed use her?

The puppy stood on his hind legs and looked up at her. She lowered her head and kissed his furry little face.

Hawk closed his eyes for a second. Ysun, help me, he thought, asking the Life Giver for strength. He wanted to be with Jenny, to give truth to the rumor about them being lovers.

He rose to his feet. "I guess I should go.''

Jenny stood, too, but she didn't release Muddy. "Can he stay and visit with me for a while?"

"Sure, but you better keep a close eye on him. He's still chewing pillows behind my back."

She laughed a little, then walked him to the door. "Thank you, Hawk."

He looked into her eyes. "For what?"

"For being honest. For telling me about your past."

"Maybe you'll tell me about yours sometime," he said.

Her posture went stiff, and he realized he'd hit a nerve. She didn't want to talk about her past. She had deep-seated secrets, and she didn't trust him enough to share them.

She really was a dove with a damaged wing, he thought. A beautiful, wounded creature struggling to fly.

"Are you free on Sunday?" he asked.

She gnawed delicately on her bottom lip, and he wondered if she knew how often she did that.

"I have the day off," she said.

"Good. So do I. Do you want to come to the Raptor House with me? I can give you a private tour." He wanted her to see the birds that guided his spirit, the hawks that had become part of him.

"All right," she said, holding Muddy close to her chest.

He smiled and reached out to pet the dog, but when he brushed Jenny's arm, she flinched.

Stunned by her reaction, he drew back.

"You startled me," she said, explaining her jumpiness.

No, he thought. It was more than that. Much more.

That unexpected uneasiness was part of her secret, he realized. Part of the wounded little bird inside her. Their mutual attraction frightened her.

Troubled, Hawk stepped back, giving her room to breathe. ''You can send Muddy back home anytime. Just put him on my patio. He'll let me know when he's ready to come in.''

She clung to the puppy. ''Okay.''

He said goodbye and walked onto the porch, but when he glanced over his shoulder, she'd already closed the door, leaving him alone and wondering what to do about her.

Five

On Sunday morning, Jenny changed her clothes three times. Finally she settled on jeans, a simple blue blouse and a pair of lace-up boots.

It was foolish, she knew, to fret about what to wear on a casual outing, but she couldn't help it.

She was nervous.

Standing in front of the mirror, she twisted her hair into a loose topknot, allowing several strands to frame her face.

Why had she agreed to accompany Hawk to the Raptor House?

Because she liked him, she told herself. And she was lonely. She needed a friend.

Oh, sure. A big, tall, muscular *male* friend. Who was she trying to kid?

No one, her mind answered. Hawk made her feel safe.

Sort of.

She frowned at her reflection and saw a pair of haunted blue eyes staring back at her. She felt safe until he touched her, until he got too close.

Then don't let him get too close. Keep your distance. Protect yourself from the danger of wanting a man again, of losing yourself to him.

Hoping she'd won that battle, she secured the last few bobby pins in her hair, reached for her purse and headed for the door. She'd agreed to meet Hawk at seven.

Because she was a few minutes early, she breathed in the dew-tipped air, taking yet another moment to calm her nerves.

Spring, she noticed, was in full bloom. Bees buzzed around newly planted flowers, and birds sang their morning songs. The rising sun shone in a cloudless sky, like a warm, brandied ball hovering in a sea of endless blue.

She walked across the lawn and waited near Hawk's truck, still caught up in her surroundings.

Jenny liked South Texas. She liked the cotton fields burgeoning in the distance, the acres of citrus groves scenting the wind.

She liked cowboy hats, cowboy boots and—

Hawk came out of his house, jarring her thoughts. He looked like a tailor-made Texan, heavily accented with an Indian flair.

He sported a denim work shirt, crisp jeans and western boots. His belt consisted of leather and hair-bone pipe, and the turquoise nugget he favored thumped against his chest.

His hair, secured in a ponytail, fell in a sleek black line down the center of his back. The talons in his ears reminded her of how he had earned his name.

Hawk Wainwright was part hawk.

And Jenny Taylor was nervous again.

"Good morning," he said when they were nearly face-to-face.

"Hi." She grabbed the base of her handbag, trying to keep her hands busy. Her palms had begun to sweat. A physical reaction, she supposed, to his rough and rugged appeal.

"You look pretty, Jenny."

"I do?" She felt her eyes widen, certain she looked more like a doe spooked by a set of glaring headlights than a woman capable of controlling her emotions.

"Yeah. The messy hair works on you."

"Oh." She went after one of the loose strands. Roy used to criticize her modern-day Gibson-girl look, discouraging her from wearing it. "Thank you," she said, grateful for the compliment. The tousled hairstyle was her rebellion, she realized, her way of defying Roy. Just like pizza with pineapple and Canadian bacon.

"Ready?" he asked.

"Yes."

He opened the truck door, and she took her seat and strapped herself in. The interior smelled like sage, and a colorful seed-beaded necklace dangled from the rearview mirror. Its multilayered strands reminded her of a tiny rainbow.

When Hawk noticed her admiring the necklace, he removed it from its mirrored perch and handed it to her. "Do you like it?"

"Yes, it's beautiful."

"Good. I bought it for you."

Her heart clogged her throat. "Why would you buy me something?"

"I don't know. I just did. If you don't want it, you don't have to keep it. I'll just leave it in the truck."

Jenny stared at the necklace. Roy used to bring her jewelry. He would hand her a perfectly wrapped box, and then with tears in his eyes, apologize for his anger and the bruises he had left on her body.

I don't know what came over me. I promise

I'll never hurt you again. You believe me, don't you, baby?

Yes, she'd believed him. More times than she could count.

She fingered the tiny beads. This gift seemed pure and genuine by comparison, a far cry from those shimmering gold trinkets reeking of heartache and brutality.

Jenny turned to see Hawk watching her.

"Thank you," she said quietly, slipping the necklace over her head.

"You're welcome," he responded just as quietly.

They drove in silence after that, passing fertile farmland and cattle ranches. Pastures went on forever, green, rich and thriving with life.

Jenny lost herself in the mood. And in the music.

The CD playing on the stereo drifted through the cab in a blend of mystery, magic and Native American flutes. She closed her eyes and imagined herself in another century, a place where peace and tranquillity floated across the plains.

It was a dream she often had, a fantasy in which Roy could never find her.

Time passed, thirty minutes or maybe an hour. Jenny continued to cling to the music, letting it filter through the fairy tale in her mind.

"Hey, sleepyhead," she heard a masculine voice say.

She opened her eyes and looked at Hawk.

How would that other century affect him? she wondered. Would he be an Apache rooted to his people? Or a mixed blood caught between two cultures, much in the same manner he was today?

"We're almost there," he told her.

She righted her posture. "I wasn't asleep." I was daydreaming, she confessed silently, feeling suddenly foolish. What good did it do to pretend that Roy didn't exist? Or that she and Hawk had traveled back in time?

Reality was what it was.

And Hawk couldn't save her from her nightmares.

He pulled into a dirt parking lot, and she unbuckled her seat belt.

The South Texas Raptor House sat on a grassy parcel of land flanked by trees and shrubs.

An unpretentious brick building housed a small office and a large supply room. Besides a refrigerator and a freezer, Jenny noticed shelves stocked with bleach, brushes, water buckets, gloves and various other items. A roughhewn table held a scale. Hawk told her it was used to check and maintain the weight of a bird.

A few minutes later they walked along a dirt path, and as Jenny looked around, he said, "It's not what you expected, is it?"

She shook her head. She'd imagined a zoo of sorts, but all she saw were rows and rows of what appeared to be large wooden sheds.

"They're called mews," he said.

Jenny learned that mews provided the bird of prey with privacy, as well as protection from vandals and stray animals. Each mews contained enough room for the raptor to stretch its wings and fly from perch to perch. A bath with fresh water was also a standard feature.

Hawk unlocked one of the mews, and Jenny discovered it had a safety chamber, an extra room with a second door that prevented birds from escaping.

"I want you to meet Hera," he said. "She's a red-tailed hawk. We take her to schools and other organizations to help educate the public."

Jenny followed Hawk into the mews, then stood in awe, studying the perched creature. The size of the bird alone was magnificent, but the mottled feathers, combined with intelligent eyes, sharp beak and powerful-looking feet took her breath away.

"Hera is an imprint," Hawk said. "She can't go back into the wild. She's been in captivity since she was a baby."

He approached the hawk with a gloved hand. "Raptors normally imprint during the period when their eyes are beginning to focus. In the wild, young birds imprint with their parents. Hera imprinted with humans, instead."

Jenny watched him attach jesses to the leather bracelets on the hawk, a method used by falconers to keep a raptor on a leash.

"She seems so tame," Jenny commented, impressed with the beauty of man and bird.

"She is. But imprinting with humans can create some dangerous behavior," he explained. "An adult bird might try to mate with a human during breeding season. Others will defend their territory against humans, the way they would defend their territory from their own species. That's why imprints can't be released into the wild."

Jenny eyed the raptor on Hawk's fist. "She doesn't exhibit dangerous behavior, does she?"

"No. But she has been known to get a little too loving, particularly with me."

"She's tried to mate with you?"

"Sort of. When she's in season, she sits on my feet

and offers me her food. She pesters me to scratch her, too. But normally we don't pet the birds.'' He smiled and headed for the safety chamber, taking Hera outside.

For a moment Jenny just stood in the mews, picturing the red-tail getting a little too loving with Hawk. Well, no wonder, she thought. After all, he was part hawk.

Once they were outdoors, Hera soaked up the sun, spreading her enormous wings and showing Jenny how regal she was. Hera had been named after the reigning Greek goddess of Olympus, a deity who took many forms, including that of a bird.

Hera folded her wings, but maintained a queenly pose. Jenny and Hawk walked along one of the dirt paths, enjoying the morning air.

''This is a small facility,'' he said. ''The center survives on donations, and everyone who works here is a volunteer.'' They passed rows of cages he called the weathering area, a place for raptors to be exposed to the elements. ''We have an adoption program where a private citizen can sponsor a particular bird. And when that bird is ready to be released, they can watch it being returned to the wild.''

''That sounds like a productive program.''

''It is.''

He turned toward her, and they gazed at each other. With the hawk riding majestically on his fist, he looked like an ancient warrior, his eyes dark and mesmerizing, his skin bronzed from the sun.

''Nothing comes close to watching a bird being returned to its natural habitat,'' he said.

She only nodded, wishing her heart wasn't pounding in her throat.

Breaking eye contact, they continued their journey, and Jenny found the strength to relax.

Twenty minutes later Hawk brought Hera back to her mews. Another volunteer, a elderly man named Sam, stopped by with a treat for the bird. Hawk thanked Sam and handed the dead mouse to Jenny.

She made a squeamish face and held the rodent by the tip of its tail. "What am I supposed to do with it?"

Hawk chuckled, clearly amused by her reaction. "Toss it to Hera. She'll catch it."

Jenny glanced at Hera. The red-tail sat on her perch, watching with keen interest.

With her face still scrunched, Jenny threw the mouse.

As fast as lightning, Hera snatched the thing with her foot, grasping it with powerful talons.

"Oh, my." Jenny had expected the bird to catch the prey in her beak.

"Raptors hunt with their feet," Hawk reminded her.

Jenny turned, and he smiled at her. She smiled back at him, and her heart skipped a beat. She hated that nervous feeling, but she liked looking at him.

"Do you want to meet Vulcan?" he asked. "He's another education bird."

"Vulcan? Like the *Star Trek* character?" Jenny asked, wondering if Vulcan was a long-eared owl. Hawk had mentioned earlier that the center had a long-eared owl, and it probably looked a bit like Mr. Spock.

"Vulcan is the Roman name for Hepahaestus," Hawk explained. "He was a lame god."

"Lame as in he bumbled his magic?"

"No. Lame as in he walked with a limp."

Once they entered Vulcan's mews, she understood why the bird had been given that name. He wasn't a long-eared owl. He was a harrier hawk, and he was lame.

Without getting too close, Jenny knelt on the pebbled floor to study him. The medium-size gray raptor sat on a ground-level perch, staring back at her.

Her emotions rose to the surface. She wanted to pet him, to comfort him in some way, but she knew she couldn't. He wasn't a domestic animal. He was a wild creature.

"He only has one wing," she said, her throat constricting.

"Yes, but to the raptor house he's still as powerful as a god." Hawk watched Jenny, thinking how fragile she seemed, far more fragile than the one-winged bird that had apparently just captured her heart.

He sat next to her, wishing he could turn her face toward his, stroke her cheek and kiss her. "Vulcan isn't an imprint. But he's used to people. He seems to enjoy being an education bird."

"How did he lose his wing?"

"It was shattered in an accident and had to be amputated." Something inside Jenny had shattered, too, he thought. Maybe that was why the one-winged harrier stirred her so deeply. "Normally amputees aren't chosen for education programs. They have a hard time maintaining their balance, especially when they bate."

"Bate?"

"Attempt to fly when they're restrained by jesses and a leash," he explained. "Vulcan does okay, though. We've spent a lot of time with him. When he falls, we help him back up.''

''He still tries to fly?'' she asked, her voice on the verge of breaking.

''It's instinct.'' Hawk had been involved in training Vulcan, and handling a damaged bird seemed far easier than touching Jenny.

Taking a chance, he rested his gloved hand on her knee. Gently, he told himself, keeping his fingertips as light as a whisper.

She didn't flinch, but her breath rushed out.

''Vulcan stayed with me for a while,'' he went on, removing his hand as cautiously as he'd applied it. He was a patient man, a man who knew how to calm skittish birds, to earn their trust. And for Hawk, it was easier to think of Jenny as a bird, even though he knew she was frightened by the attraction that hummed between them. ''I perched him everywhere. In front of the TV. In the kitchen when the dishwasher was running. He adjusted to the noise and movement. Vulcan doesn't get stressed anymore.''

To prove his point, he attached a lease to Vulcan's jesses and coached the harrier onto his fist. As Hawk stood, Jenny did, too.

It was the most important display he'd ever made, an emotional display for an emotional woman. He wanted to ask who had hurt her, but he didn't know how to pose a question like that, so he moved a little closer, instead.

''I think Vulcan likes you,'' he said.

''Really?'' She blinked and smiled at the bird.

''I like you, too,'' he added. ''But I feel as if I barely know you. You're so secretive, Jenny.''

She dropped her gaze. ''I don't mean to be.''

"I know. But if you ever want to talk, I'm willing to listen. It's not good to keep things bottled up inside."

She crossed her arms protectively, still avoiding eye contact. "I appreciate your concern, but I can handle what's going on in my life. And I'd rather not get you involved."

"Okay." He backed off, realizing he didn't have much of a choice. If he pushed too hard, he would lose her.

And Hawk didn't want to lose her. Their friendship was too important to him. And so was the warmth and desire she made him feel.

The attraction that made her much too wary.

Late that night, while the moon shimmered in the sky, Jenny awoke with a scream.

Not a death-defying shriek, but a muffled cry, the sound she made whenever she dreamed of Roy, when his hands choked the very breath from her lungs.

Reaching for her pillow, she clutched it to her chest, then scooted against the wall, gulping for the air she'd lost.

In her dream, Roy had found her. He'd hidden in her house, lurking in the shadows like a snake. And when he'd grabbed her, she'd tried to fight him off, but he was too strong.

Dear God. She'd let him kill her. She'd let him—

"No," Jenny whispered. She hadn't let him squeeze the life out of her. She was still breathing.

But someday she wouldn't be. Someday her recurring nightmare would come true.

Wide-eyed, she looked around in the darkness. He could be out there right now, waiting to strike.

So do something.

What? she asked herself. Call the sheriff?

No. He'd just think she was a hysterical female. The police couldn't protect her from a nightmare.

Cautious, she climbed out of bed and tiptoed to the closet for her robe, refusing to switch on the lamp. If Roy was out there, he might be able to see her through the blinds, like a Peeping Tom peering into an illuminated window.

Belting the terry robe around her, she prayed for an answer, something to take away the fear.

Silence swirled like a ghost. And then an answer slipped into her mind.

She could call Hawk. She could tell him that she'd had a nightmare. Hawk had offered to listen, to be there when she needed someone to talk to.

Jenny glanced at the digital clock. Two twenty-two. What would he think if he got a call from his female neighbor at two in the morning?

Tanya used to call him in the middle of the night. But not because she was frightened. Tanya had wanted sex.

Jenny tightened her robe.

No way would she call him. She would stay up all night if she had to, waiting for the sun to rise, but she wouldn't rouse Hawk from his bed.

Jenny squinted into the dark. If she could just find the strength to forget about her dream, turn on the light and go into the kitchen for a cup of hot choc olate.

She needed something to soothe her nerves. Something to take the edge—

The telephone shrieked eerily.

Oh, my God! her mind screamed. She stood dead still, her frantic heart clamoring in her chest.

It was Roy.

No, she told herself, struggling to temper the panic. He wouldn't call. He wouldn't warn her that he was nearby. Roy would sneak in with the shadows.

The phone continued to peal, a reminder that she wasn't alone. Someone had dialed her number.

In the middle of the night.

What if *was* Roy? What if he—

It stopped ringing, leaving her with nothing but the chill of silence.

Jenny fumbled for the slim silver flashlight in her bottom drawer, pushing through folded clothes to find it.

The phone started up again.

She shone the silver beacon on it, illuminating the plastic with a harsh, circular beam.

Don't let it taunt you, damn it. Answer it.

Still clutching the flashlight, she picked up the receiver, but didn't speak. Instead, she waited for the caller to announce himself.

"Jenny?"

Oh, God.

"It's me, honey. Hawk. Are you okay?"

Her knees liquefied. She sank onto the bed, tears flooding her eyes.

"Please, Jenny, say something. Answer me."

"I'm all right."

"But you were awake. You were afraid."

"Yes." How did he know? How could he possibly know?

"I'm coming over," he said. "I just have to throw on some jeans." He paused, and she thought she heard the roll of a sliding closet door. "I'll be there in a minute."

"Okay." Her hand shook so badly the silver beacon flickered like a strobe light, giving the pitch-black room an unearthly glow.

When she answered the knock at the front door, Hawk stood on the porch, just staring at her.

She stared back.

Suddenly she didn't know what frightened her more—her dream or the fact that Hawk had somehow known she was afraid.

"Please tell me it was all right that I called," he said.

It had to be all right, she told herself. He wasn't Roy. "I don't understand how you knew."

"I had a dream, Jenny. I dreamed that you were afraid."

She could see the moon behind him. A slash of its pearly glow glinted off his hair. His shirt wasn't buttoned, and his jeans were barely zipped. His feet, she noticed, stood bare.

His eyes shone like burning coals, and the talons in his ears had their own haunting magic. He didn't look like her protector, but he must be.

At least for tonight.

"I debated on whether or not I should call," he said, still seeking for her approval.

"Come in," she offered, her voice just above a whisper.

He stepped into her living room, and she wondered if his feet were damp and cold.

Jenny couldn't think straight. She couldn't think beyond the confusion.

"I need to sit down." She made it to the couch

before her legs gave way. Her bones were melting into slush.

"Now that I'm here, I don't know what to do." He watched her through those coal-black eyes. "You're not one of my birds."

She looked up at him. The statement struck her as odd, but she didn't question him. Breathing deeply, she pulled air into her oxygen-deprived lungs.

"Did we have the same dream?" she asked.

"I don't know." He sat beside her. "In my dream you were alone and afraid. You were walking through a mist, and the mist was choking you."

Jenny closed her eyes. "There wasn't any mist in my dream."

"But you were suffocating, weren't you?"

"Yes."

"Why?" he asked as she opened her eyes.

"Because someone had their hands around my throat."

"Who?" He didn't move closer, but she saw his body shift.

She didn't respond. She felt queasy, a little dizzy. She prayed she wouldn't faint in his arms again.

"Jenny?" he pressed. "Don't shut me out. Not now."

"It was Roy," she managed.

Hawk's gaze locked on hers. "Who's Roy? Who is he?"

"My ex-husband," she said. "And someday he's going to kill me."

Six

"Tell me about Roy," Hawk said, his voice rough. "I want to know everything."

When she didn't answer, he softened his tone. "Don't worry, honey. I won't let him hurt you."

Jenny's mouth went dry. How could Hawk protect her? He wasn't her bodyguard. He couldn't be with her night and day. "You can't stop him from coming after me."

"I can sure as hell try."

She shook her head. She had no right to involve Hawk, to expect him to rescue her.

"Let me get you some water," he said as she wet her lips. "And then we'll talk."

He went into the kitchen and she heard him opening cupboards until he found the glasses. Her kitchen was just like his, but apparently she'd arranged it differently.

He returned with ice water and handed it to her. Grateful for the drink, she sipped slowly. The nausea had passed, but she was still a little dizzy.

Hawk sat beside her again, his eyes dark and intense.

She placed the glass on a nearby table. Who was this man? And how did he slip into her subconscious?

"Do you always get such strong feelings in your dreams?" she asked.

"I've never had a dream that involved someone else, at least not to the degree this one did. But dreams are significant in my culture, and I couldn't ignore the connection between us. That's why I called. I knew you were frightened."

A chill crept up her spine. "Because the dream is going to come true."

"No, it isn't. He isn't going to lay a hand on you, Jenny. Do you hear me? I won't let him."

"You don't know what he's like. How dangerous he is." She clutched her stomach. She could still feel the cramping and the bleeding, the horrible, frightening loss. "Roy killed our baby. I was eight weeks pregnant, and he shoved me against a wall, over and over again. A few hours later, I miscarried."

"Dear God," Hawk whispered.

"I still think about the baby." She still prayed for its tiny soul every night before she went to bed. "When it first happened, Roy said he was sorry. He said he'd do anything to make it up to me. But after I filed for divorce, he refused to take responsibility. His sorrow turned to anger."

Hawk frowned, and Jenny took a deep breath, gaining the strength to talk about the past, to tell him about the man she had married.

"I met Roy right after I graduated from college. I was twenty-two and I thought he was the most charming, sophisticated man in the world. He owned a travel agency, and I was just a small-town girl."

She paused, recalling how naive she had been. "I wasn't born in Salt Lake City. I came from a quiet little community in Utah, and I had stars in my eyes. I wanted to be rich and successful, the kind of woman who could rule her own destiny." She held Hawk's gaze, even though the distress she saw in his eyes made her uncomfortable. It was odd telling one man about another. "I knew I had talent, and as focused as I was on my career, I was just as focused on Roy."

"I'm having a hard time with this," he said. "Your husband was a bastard, Jenny."

"But I didn't know that. When we were first married, he seemed like the perfect partner. He was attentive and kind. He showered me with attention. And he took me on trips. We traveled to so many exotic locations."

"There weren't any warning signs? Nothing that indicated his true character?"

Yes, she thought, the signs were there. "He was possessive, almost to the point of obsession, and he would get upset when other men looked at me. But I wanted to please him, to prove that I was a loyal wife, so I allowed him to control me, to choose my wardrobe and dictate whom I socialized with."

She took a breath and forced herself to go on. "Roy is ten years older than me, and I assumed there was just a generation gap between us, that he was insecure because of my youth." She heaved a weary sigh. "I made excuses for him. I told myself it didn't matter that he was molding me into the kind of woman he thought I should be, rather than letting me mature on my own. He was older and wiser and more experienced. I respected his opinion."

"And you loved him?"

"Yes. I loved him more than anything."

Hawk couldn't imagine being loved so deeply. He couldn't imagine a woman as pure and beautiful as Jenny giving him her heart.

How could Roy hurt her? How could he take all that beauty and maim it?

"When did he first turn violent?" Hawk asked.

"About a year after we were married, he slapped me. He was angry because I had come home late from a business meeting, and I'd forgotten to call." She paused to touch the side of her face. "Afterward he took me in his arms and begged for my forgiveness. I was so confused. He seemed so sincere, so remorseful."

"So you forgave him?"

"I didn't know what else to do. He was my husband, and I truly believed that he loved me, that he would never hurt me again."

Hawk frowned. "But he did."

She nodded. "Yes."

"Then why did you stay?"

"There were so many reasons. Misguided hope, fear. I can't explain it. I wanted to walk away, but I couldn't." She twisted the belt on her robe. "And when my mother fell ill, I knew I had to stay. Roy helped me place her in a nursing home. I was still establishing my career, but Roy's business earned enough to provide her with the best medical care available."

Hawk drew a ragged breath. Jenny looked so damn vulnerable, he thought. So pale. Her night-tousled hair tangled around her face, and shadows rimmed her eyes.

"My dad died when I was a little," she said. "And Mom was a quiet, trusting woman. To her, Roy was everything he appeared to be. He was the white knight and I was his princess. She was so proud of us." Jenny's eyes glazed with tears. "I couldn't bear to tell her the truth. And if I left Roy, how was I going to pay for her care?''

Hawk didn't know what to say. He couldn't begin to understand what Jenny had lived through. He'd heard of Battered Woman's Syndrome, but he didn't know what it meant, exactly. Now he did.

"No one knew what was going on? Not your friends or co-workers?''

She shook her head. "If my arms were bruised, I wore long sleeves to cover them. He never broke my nose or blackened my eye. Nothing obvious.''

"But he pushed you so hard, you lost your baby.''

She gulped audibly. "When I discovered I was pregnant, Roy was thrilled. He said a child was just what we needed. I was happy, too. I wanted so desperately to be a mother. And Roy stopped hurting me. He was back to being a kind, caring husband.''

Her voice broke a little, but she continued, "I thought the baby had changed him. But one Sunday, he lost his temper and started shoving me against the kitchen wall, nearly knocking me unconscious. That's when I miscarried.''

Hawk wanted to castrate Roy, to unman the son of a bitch with a sharp, cold blade.

Jenny twisted the belt on her robe again. The fabric was soft and fluffy, and it made her look even more delicate.

"Did you tell your mother?'' he asked.

"No. She died right after I lost the baby. Her illness had progressed and…''

When Jenny's tears began to fall, Hawk wished he could hold her. But he wasn't sure if she would welcome his touch. "I'm so sorry.''

She swiped at her tears. "I divorced Roy, but I had

to leave Salt Lake City to get away from him. He stalked me once, and he'll do it again. I know he's looking for me.''

And if he finds you, I'll kill him, Hawk thought. ''Come on, honey. Why don't you go back to bed? You need to sleep.''

''Will you stay?'' she asked. ''On the couch,'' she added, her cheeks flushing a little. ''There are sheets in the linen closet.''

''No problem. I can hang around all day if you need me to. I work for myself. My schedule is flexible.'' And he couldn't bear to leave her alone. He offered her his hand. ''Let me tuck you in.''

''You don't have to do that.''

''I want to,'' he persisted.

She agreed quietly. Taking his hand, she allowed him to help her up, but she broke contact once she was on her feet.

He followed her down the hall.

Jenny's room was decorated in pastels and blond woods. An eyelet comforter dominated the unmade bed, and a floral scent drifted through the air.

He spotted a crystal bowl filled with the flower petals he'd envisioned earlier.

She removed her robe, revealing a modest nightgown. The white garment, adorned with lavender ribbon, flowed to her ankles.

She climbed into bed, and he adjusted the covers around her.

Her gold-streaked hair and pale skin made her look like an angel tortured by demons.

Sweet, fragile Jenny.

''Thank you,'' she whispered, closing her eyes.

''You're welcome,'' he responded just as softly.

He watched her for a moment, then headed for the couch.

Soon he'd make some inquiries about Roy, check on the other man's whereabouts. Hawk intended to protect Jenny, but he needed to know more about the son of a bitch who had her running scared.

When Jenny awakened, bright light filtered through the blinds. She sat up and squinted at the clock. It was afternoon.

She reached for her robe, wondering how Hawk had slept. She'd slept soundly, knowing he had been nearby.

Feeling a little awkward, she headed for the living room. What would they say to each other now that sun was up? She didn't want to talk about Roy or the tears she'd shed last night.

Hawk sat on the edge of the couch, rubbing his hands over his face. His chest was bare, and his hair fell in disarray.

For a moment she just stood, watching him.

He looked sleepy. Sexy. And much too male.

When he glanced up, she did her darnedest to act casual.

"Hi," she said.

"Hi," he repeated her greeting in a graveled voice. Did he feel awkward, too?

He must, she decided. He remained as quiet as she. But then, sleeping under the same roof seemed strangely intimate.

"Did you just wake up?" she asked.

"Yeah." His voice scratched sensuously over her skin. "Did you?"

She nodded and rubbed her arms.

He stood and reached for his discarded sheet, and they both fell silent.

He looked big and masculine in the feminine surroundings. She hadn't decorated with a man in mind. In fact, she'd done just the opposite.

Glancing at the sheet Hawk was attempting to fold, she bit back a smile. The tiny-rosebud print didn't suit him very well, not with that massive chest and those bulging biceps.

He tossed the hastily folded sheet aside, and she lost the urge to smile. She could feel her nipples budding beneath her nightgown. The flex of male muscle actually aroused her.

"Is it all right if I use your bathroom?" he asked.

"Of course."

"Thanks." When he passed her, she watched him walk down the hall.

He closed the bathroom door, and she wondered if he would remember to put the toilet seat down.

Heavens, it felt strange to have a man in her house.

Jenny tried to clear her thoughts. Imagining him in her bathroom was a stupid thing to do. He wasn't moving in. He was her neighbor, a friend she'd confided in.

The rumors about them weren't true. They weren't lovers, and in spite of their mutual attraction, they weren't on the verge of becoming lovers.

Jenny wasn't ready to allow a man access to her body. Nor was she capable of giving someone her heart.

Being stingy kept her safe.

She hadn't told Hawk everything about Roy. There was one humiliating secret she couldn't possibly share.

Hawk returned and found her standing in the same spot.

"Are you okay?" he asked.

"I'm fine."

"Are you sure? You look like you were thinking about something important."

"I wasn't," she responded. "I'm still a little sleepy, I guess."

"I was thinking about a shower." He pulled his hand across his jaw. "And a shave. I should go home and get cleaned up. Plus, I need to let Muddy out. Do you want me to come back, or would you rather be alone?"

She realized he was trying hard to accommodate her, to be the kind of friend she needed. But it wasn't easy, she supposed. Their gender difference got in the way.

"I'd like you to come back," she answered honestly. "You can take my keys to let yourself in. You know, in case I'm in the shower." She needed to bathe, too. And her regimen might take longer than his.

He smiled and grabbed his shirt off the coffee table. "Okay."

She handed him the keys, wondering if she should make him a spare. Or would that seem like an open invitation, an offer between lovers rather than friends?

He stuffed the keys in his pocket, but he didn't put on the wrinkled shirt. Instead, he left her house just the way he was, clad in nothing but a pair of faded jeans.

He looked as if he'd just tumbled out of a woman's warm, willing bed. And that, she realized, was exactly what every neighbor who saw him would assume.

There was no point in trying to deny the rumors now. Who would believe he'd slept on the couch?

Jenny picked up the sheet he'd used, resisting the girlish impulse to press the fabric against her body.

Feminine arousal was the last thing she needed to contend with.

Then take a shower and cool off, she told herself. Quit thinking about him like that.

Jenny entered the bathroom, grateful the tiny room seemed the same. Hawk hadn't made his masculine presence known. He hadn't forgotten to put the toilet seat down.

Ten minutes later she emerged from the shower and found a suitable outfit for lounging around the house with a friend. Rather than taking the time to blow-dry her hair, she secured it in a ponytail with a big gold barrette.

Next she went into the kitchen and opened the fridge, searching for something to fix for breakfast. Or lunch, she supposed, given the hour.

Jenny went for ham and eggs. She was in the mood for an omelet.

Just as she cracked the first egg, Muddy skidded into the room, giving her a start.

Hawk was back.

She looked up to see him leaning in the doorway. This time he wore a shirt, but that didn't diminish his appeal.

"I hope you don't mind having an omelet for lunch," she said.

"Not at all." He shifted his gaze to the dog. "Muddy, knock it off."

Jenny glanced down and nearly tripped over the puppy. Seated on his rear, with his two front paws in the air, he begged at her feet. "Oh, my goodness. Where did he learn to do that?"

"I don't know, but he does it all the time. It was cute at first, but he's turning into a ham."

Ham, she realized, was exactly what the pup was after. "Do you mind if I feed him?"

"I guess not. He never eats his dog food, anyway."

Jenny had to laugh. As tough as Hawk pretended to be, he let Muddy get away with all sorts of mischievous behavior.

She dropped a slice of meat to the dog. He caught it in one swift bite.

She dropped him another one. And then another. He didn't tire of the begging position; he remained at her feet, poised prettily.

"Okay, that's enough." This came from Hawk.

The puppy woofed back at him, and Hawk shook his head.

"Don't take that tone with me. You're making a nuisance of yourself. Jenny will think you don't have any manners."

Muddy barked again, then gazed at Jenny with big blameless eyes.

She gave him another slice of ham.

Hawk moved in beside her. "Do I have to beg for my meal, too? Or does that only work for spoiled dogs?"

She turned to look at him and realized how close he was. She could smell his aftershave, and she could see the teasing affection in his eyes.

Jenny didn't know what to do. That uncomfortable electricity between them had come back, the tingling sensation, the carnal warmth she wasn't ready to face.

Her nipples pressed against her bra, pushing clean

through to her T-shirt. All Hawk had to do was glance down to see the kind of effect he was having on her.

She wondered if he was aroused, too.

"There's plenty of ham," she said inanely.

His lips twitched into a smile. "So I don't have to beg?"

"No." Why couldn't she smile back at him? Why couldn't she relax?

Because he'd spent the night. Because she'd pictured him in her bathroom. Because he made her nipples hard.

As if on cue, he dropped his gaze.

Jenny prayed he wouldn't notice.

His eyes shot back to hers. And they stared at each other, their gazes locked in a sexual pull.

He'd noticed.

What should I do? she asked herself. What should I say to ease the tension?

He moved even closer. Close enough to kiss.

Jenny struggled to maintain her composure. Her knees went foolishly weak, and a sprig of warmth spread through her body, heating the pit of her stomach. She inhaled the spicy scent of his aftershave, the fragrance projecting his power.

Nervous, she waited, debating her options.

Push him away.

Let the kiss happen.

Tell him no.

Say yes.

Suddenly the notion gave her power. Yes. No. The choice was hers. Roy wasn't here, dictating her every move.

Hawk stepped back and cleared his throat. "I'm sorry, Jenny."

No, she thought, don't apologize. Let me decide if I want to kiss you.

"I'm really sorry," he said again. "I didn't mean to put you in that position."

The adrenaline drained from her body like air from a punctured balloon.

Avoiding eye contact, she glanced down and saw that Muddy had given up on her, too. The dog sniffed around the kitchen floor, searching for tidbits.

Hawk had actually apologized. Like the patron saint of abused women.

That made her feel useless and unwanted.

Jenny looked up and caught Hawk watching her. Who was his last lover? she wondered. A beautiful, young Native American? Someone eager to please him?

He wasn't as saintly as he seemed. He was a man—flesh and blood and full of hunger. When he needed a woman, he would find one.

And Jenny had no right to feel this blast of envy.

But damn, she did. And now she was angry that he'd treated her like a splintered piece of glass.

"Why did you apologize?" she asked, piercing that midnight gaze of his.

For a moment Hawk could only stare. "Because…"

"Because why?" she pressed.

"You're afraid of me. You're afraid of the way I make you feel."

She lifted her chin in a stubborn gesture, and if he hadn't been reeling from need, her spunk would have amused him. He'd wanted to kiss her, to push his tongue into her mouth and run his hands all over her body.

His arousal tented his jeans, and her nipples protruded like bullets. But that didn't mean she could handle what was happening between them.

"I'm not afraid of a kiss," she said, sounding tougher than she looked.

"Aren't you?" He'd seen the indecision in her eyes, the feminine want edged with fear. To prove his point, he moved toward her. And he kept moving until he'd pinned her against the counter.

Her breath rushed out. "What are you doing?"

"Showing you how much I want you." In one fluid motion he ran his hands down her back, cupped her bottom and brought her body to his, heat to blazing heat.

Her entire body shivered.

He dipped his head and nuzzled her ear. "You're excited, but you're afraid." He could feel her heartbeat, the jittery pounding, the erratic stumble. "I don't want to kiss you when you're afraid."

"What about what I want? I'm tired of men making decisions for me."

"I'm not trying to make decisions for you, but it's obvious you need time to heal." He released her, but didn't step back. His heart was pounding, too. And if she had been anyone but Jenny, he would have tangled his hands into her hair, pulled her against him and kissed her breathless.

"I'm not a piece of glass, Hawk. Don't treat me like I'm about to shatter."

But she was, he realized. She was on the brink of breaking, of smashing into a thousand jagged pieces. She had no idea how fragile she was. Or how dangerously close he was to dragging her back into his arms.

"Let's make a deal," he said. "When you want me, you can have me."

She blinked. "What's that supposed to mean?"

"It means I'm yours for the taking. You can kiss me if you feel like it. Hell, you can unzip my pants and slide your hands—"

She gasped, and he grinned. He'd certainly gotten her attention. "There's no rush, Jenny. I'll be here when you're ready."

"What if I'm not ready for a really long time?"

He roamed his gaze over her. God, she was beautiful. The afternoon light shined through the window, giving her a sun-kissed halo. He knew their attraction confused her. Hell, it confused him, too.

"I'll wait until you make the first move," he said. "No matter how long it takes."

"You won't go to another woman?"

The question startled him, but he feigned a casual air. Did she realize they were making a commitment? That they'd crossed the friendship line?

"No."

"No what?"

"No, I won't go to another woman." Did she really think he had a choice? She was in his blood now. She was the woman he craved.

He moistened his lips, his body still humming with arousal. "So, do we have a deal?"

She gave him a serious study. Too serious. He felt her gaze everywhere, observing him like a butcher analyzing a side of beef.

Suddenly worried, he sucked in his nonexistent gut. Maybe she'd changed her mind about him. Maybe she—

"Okay," she said.

He shifted his stance. "Okay what?"

"Okay, we have a deal."

Hawk released the air from his lungs. Jenny had just accepted his unusual offer, but that didn't change the facts. He knew damn well she wouldn't be kissing him today.

She needed time.

And there was nothing he could do but wait.

Seven

Jenny cracked the last egg into a glass bowl and picked up the whisk. Hawk stood a few feet away from her, grating cheese. Muddy, the charming beggar, had been banished to the patio.

Careful not to bump Hawk's shoulder, Jenny made her way to the fridge. The kitchen was barely big enough for two, but he'd insisted on helping with the meal.

She removed the milk, and he turned to look at her.

Instantly something tangled in her stomach.

Nerves, she realized.

He still made her nervous.

Well, no wonder. He'd invited her to unzip his pants and slide her hands inside.

Adding a dash of milk to the eggs, she did her best to avoid looking at his fly, to keep her eyes above his waist. But her gaze strayed.

"It's ready," he said.

Her eyes flew back up to his face. "I'm sorry. What?"

He motioned to the grated cheddar. "The cheese."

"Oh, yes. Of course."

"Is there something else I can do?" he asked.

"This needs to be diced." Jenny gave him the ham, then slipped past him for a diversion, checking on the hash browns. After lifting the lid, she added another dash of paprika.

Twenty minutes later, they sat across from each other at her whitewashed table.

The scent of breakfast wafted through the air.

He buttered his toast, and she analyzed her situation.

So what if Hawk still made her nervous? She had agreed to the arrangement he'd suggested, and for good reason. It would give her the opportunity to execute the independence Roy had stolen from her—to make decisions, to control her own destiny.

If she wanted Hawk, she could kiss him.

He cut into his omelet and took a bite. "Do you ride?" he asked.

Jenny looked up just as he licked his lips. He meant horses, didn't he? Certainly he wasn't referring to men.

As an image of straddling him clouded her mind, her face grew warm. She'd actually asked him not to go to another woman, and he'd agreed.

"I rode when I was in college," she said.

He reached for his coffee. She noticed he took it black. She preferred cream and lots of sugar in hers. And to keep her hands busy, she added another heaping spoonful.

"Why did you stop?" he asked.

The answer disturbed her, but she told him, anyway. "Roy was jealous."

He gave her an incredulous look. "Of what? The horses?"

"No, of the men who worked at the stable where I used to ride. He thought I had a thing for cowboys. But I don't. I mean, I didn't," she corrected.

His lips curved into a boyish smile. "You didn't then, but you do now?"

Feeling shy, she shrugged. "Most women think outdoorsy men are appealing." Eager to get the subject back to horses, not the men who rode them, she said, "I checked out the stable at the Lone Star Country Club. Maybe I'll start riding there."

Hawk's smile fell. "I didn't know you were a member of the club."

Shoot. She'd just tripped herself up, but she couldn't very well backtrack now. "I'm not. But I still have access to the stable."

"Why? Because of Archy?"

She nodded. She had no recourse but to speak honestly. "He suggested a Wainwright mount."

Hawk's eyes turned cold. "As opposed to what? One of my horses?"

"No. As opposed to a Carson mount."

"Oh, yeah. That stupid feud." He frowned at his plate. "I guess you'd rather ride at the club, anyway."

"I'd rather ride with you," she said, hoping to ease his hurt. "But the horses you train belong to your clients."

He lifted his gaze. "Not all of them do. I'm a trader, too. I buy and sell. And I've got plenty of stock available."

"So I can ride with you?"

"Yeah." He grinned at her. "How about next Sunday? We can make a day of it. Pack a picnic or something."

"Okay." Her heart fluttered like a wing.

He moved his fork around. "I'm sorry for getting

upset. But your relationship with Archy still bugs me."

"I wish he could see you through my eyes. He has no idea what kind of man you are."

"I don't care what he thinks. Hell, the way Archy and I feel about each other, I should have been born a Carson."

Jenny sighed. "Do you really think the feud is stupid?" she asked, recalling how bitter Archy seemed about the Carsons.

"I don't know. I can see how it happened, I suppose."

"Will you tell me about it?" She had never heard the entire story, and she was curious about how the quarrel began.

"I can give you the condensed version. Otherwise, we'll be here for days."

Jenny's eyes widened. "There's that much bad blood between them?"

"Hell, yes. But this is how it started." Hawk sat back in his chair. "In 1898 Big Bill Carson and J.P. Wainwright met on a cattle-buying trip and became close friends. Over the years their ranches grew and prospered. Eventually their land boundaries touched, and they became neighbors." He sipped his coffee and continued, "They started throwing lavish parties, with guests coming from all over Texas and beyond. So in 1923 they decided to form a social club. Both of them deeded a thousand acres to their new venture."

"And that's how the Lone Star Country Club was formed?"

"Yes, but five years later there was trouble. Carson's eldest son, Jace, and Wainwright's only daughter, Lou Lou, fell in love, and everyone expected them to get married. But Jace got drunk one night and ended up in bed with another woman.''

Jenny made a face. "Jace was a dog."

Hawk lifted a brow. "You're taking sides already."

"He cheated."

"True, but he paid dearly for it. The other woman got pregnant, and Jace agreed to marry her. But he was still crazy in love with Lou Lou Wainwright and hating himself for what he'd done."

"Too bad," she said, not feeling the least bit sorry for Jace. "What happened to Lou Lou?"

"She committed suicide."

Jenny's heart dropped. "Oh, how awful."

"Yeah. And here's the irony—the other woman wasn't even pregnant by Jace. She'd duped him."

"What a mess."

"No kidding. But it gets worse. After Lou Lou killed herself, Papa Wainwright went gunning for Jace, but shot his old friend, Big Bill Carson, instead. Big Bill didn't die, but he ended up in a wheelchair."

"And I imagine the next generation of Carsons and Wainwrights had their fair share of problems, too."

"They sure did. And so did the generation after that."

Which brought them to the present, Jenny thought.

A moment of silence ensued. Hawk resumed eating, and she squeezed ketchup onto her hash browns.

"Do you know the Carsons very well?" she asked.

"No. But about a month ago Flynt Carson paid me a visit. He questioned me about a kidnapped baby."

She put the ketchup down and waited for him to explain.

"Last year an infant was left at the country club. Flynt and some of his buddies found her near the ninth tee. She had a note attached to her that said something like 'I'm your baby girl. My name is Lena.' But the part of the note identifying the father was damaged. So Flynt brought Lena to the Carson ranch, where she was eventually kidnapped."

"Why did he question you about it?"

"He and his wife were taking care of the kid, and when somebody nabbed her, they blamed the Wainwrights. And since I'm a Wainwright enemy, Flynt thought I might be able to help. But there wasn't anything I could tell him. I don't keep tabs on Archy and his brood."

She shook her head. "Your father has his faults, but he wouldn't kidnap an innocent child for revenge."

"I suppose not. Given the nature of that feud, Flynt jumped to conclusions."

Jenny couldn't help but worry about the child. "Have they found her?"

"No, not yet."

"Has anyone figured out who her father is?"

"Yes, but Flynt didn't tell me his name."

"What about the mother? Does anyone know who she is?"

"No, but I suspect she's in some kind of trouble. Why else would she abandon her daughter?"

Instantly Jenny thought about the baby she'd lost. She touched her stomach, recalling the tiny life that had nestled there. The life Roy had destroyed. She couldn't imagine what Lena's mother must be going through. The fear. The anxiety. The tears she must cry every night.

"Do you want another cup of coffee?" Hawk asked. "I'm getting a refill."

"No. Thanks."

He paused on his way to the counter. "Are you okay, Jenny? You look sad."

"I'm just thinking about babies."

He met her gaze from across the room, his dark eyes gentle. "You'll have other babies someday."

"I'm not too keen on getting married again," she admitted.

"That's understandable, but once you get a handle on the past, you might feel differently."

"What about you?" she asked. "Do you plan on having children?"

For a moment he only looked at her. And then he frowned. "I don't think so. It's not that I don't like kids. I'm just such a loner and…"

She nodded, comprehending his concern. His heirs would be the unwanted Wainwright grandchildren, and he couldn't bear to see them suffer the way he had.

He turned away to get the coffee, and she watched him, wishing she could make Archy care about his Apache son.

On Wednesday morning as Jenny headed for her car, she saw Hawk unlocking his truck.

Their driveways were side by side, but she and Hawk rarely ran into each other before work. He normally started his day much earlier than she did.

Had he awoken late? she wondered. Or had he changed his schedule?

He turned and spotted her, and she smoothed her dress self-consciously. She'd been thinking about him for the past two nights, wondering when she would summon the courage to kiss him.

She could do it right now. She could move closer, put her arms around him, coax his mouth to hers.

But when she took a step toward him, her courage faltered. He looked big and powerful, and much too dangerous.

"Where are you going?" he asked.

"To the club. I have an appointment this morning."

He scanned the length of her, and she hoped he liked what he saw. She'd paired the delicate Indian necklace he'd given her with a slim white dress.

As he took in her attire, she took in his. She couldn't help but notice the chain-stitched Western shirt, the leather-laced belt, the black jeans and ebony boots.

He wasn't dressed for breaking horses. He looked like a business-minded cowboy today, with his contemporary Stetson and sterling-and-turquoise watch.

"Where are you going?" she asked.

"To the city to see a private investigator. I wasn't going to mention it until after I spoke to him, but—" he paused to adjust his hat, tipping it up a notch "—I plan on hiring a P.I. to keep an eye on Roy."

Stunned, Jenny searched his gaze. She didn't know what to say, so she studied him, instead.

"I figured if you knew what Roy was up to, you'd be able to sleep better," he told her.

"I can't believe you'd do that for me."

"I want you to feel safe."

"But it's going to be expensive," she protested.

His lips thinned in a stubborn scowl. "I can handle it."

Jenny shook her head. She couldn't let him take financial responsibility for her. She would find a way to contribute, even if her funds were sorely limited. During their divorce, Roy had destroyed almost everything she owned. She'd had to replace clothes, accessories, sheets, towels, dishes, a computer.

She glanced back at her house. Although she'd decorated for style and comfort, she'd only leased the furniture, just in case she had to escape in the middle of the night and leave it all behind.

"I'll help you cover the bill," she said.

"No way." Pride shone in his eyes. "This was my idea, and I'll pay for it."

"It doesn't seem right."

"Damn it, Jenny. I'm doing this whether you like it or not." He stood rigid and tough, warning her not to argue further. He'd taken charge and he wouldn't back down.

"Thank you," she said, accepting his offer as a gift, the most special gift anyone had ever given her. "I didn't know men like you existed." Warriors, she thought. Protectors.

"You deserve some peace, Jenny."

She swallowed the lump in her throat.

They stood silently until she said, "Your P.I. will need to know that Roy's last name isn't Taylor. It's Segal. His company is called Segal Travel, and he lives on Reef Drive." In a luxurious three-story house that had become her prison. "When I came to Texas, I changed my last name to Taylor. I tell people it's my maiden name, but it's not. I was born Jennifer Lynn Evans, but I decided not to use Evans because I was afraid Roy would be able to trace me from it too easily."

"My birth name is Anthony Archibald Wainwright."

"Hawk suits you better."

"Just like Jenny suits you."

Silence stretched between them again. Sweet, awkward silence, she thought. It felt strange. A little confusing.

"I'll probably also need to give the P.I. the names and numbers of some of your old acquaintances," he said.

"That's fine. Do you want me to make up a list now?"

"Could you? It would probably speed things along."

She went back into the house and checked her address book, writing down the information he'd requested. All of her old acquaintances were people she'd worked with in some capacity. She hadn't had anyone in Salt Lake that she could consider a friend. Roy had seen to that.

When she returned, Hawk was still standing beside his truck. She gave him the names and numbers, and he folded them into his front pocket.

"I should get going," he said. I don't want to be late."

"Okay." She stepped back and sent him a shy smile, thinking how incredible he was. "I'll see you later."

He nodded. "I'll let you know what the P.I. says."

They went their separate ways. He climbed into his truck and backed out of the driveway, and she got in her car, suddenly worried about what the future might bring.

What would happen if she panicked under pressure? If she couldn't relax in Hawk's arms? If his embrace reminded her of the last time she'd been with Roy?

Or what if she disappointed Hawk? What if she didn't live up to his expectations?

Jenny's pulse shot up. She wasn't good at intimacy. She wasn't good at touching and feeling, at having a man's weight pin her to the bed.

The urge to flee had her gripping the steering wheel. And then she recalled what Hawk had said the other day.

I'm not trying to make decisions for you, but it's obvious you need time to heal.

Yes, she needed time. And by God, she would take it.

For once in her life she wouldn't rush into a relationship.

When Jenny arrived at the Lone Star Country Club, her pulse was steady, her breathing calm. She entered the Yellow Rose Café, where she'd arranged to meet the proprietor of Deacon Antiques.

The hostess approached her. "Are you Jenny Taylor?"

"Yes, I am."

"A lady named Liz Deaton called and said she was going to be a little late. She tried to reach you at home, but she didn't catch you in time."

"That's fine. I don't mind waiting."

The café was nearly empty. She sat in a sunny booth and ordered a cup of tea from Daisy.

The waitress looked tired, as if her sleep had been plagued with restlessness.

Jenny had heard that Daisy was from the wrong

side of the tracks, yet something about her spoke of an unusual and exotic elegance.

Jenny sensed there was more to Daisy Parker than met the eye.

As Daisy left to fill the order, Jenny glanced out the window and saw a white bird light on a rustic garden bench.

She studied the scene as if it were a painting, a watercolor created just for her. A sea of pink flowers swayed among leafy plants and weeping vines, like ballerinas dancing on waves of green.

Fascinated, she placed her hand against the glass. A moment later the bird took flight and disappeared in a flurry of magic.

When Daisy came back, Jenny turned to look at her. For a moment their eyes met and held, and then Daisy placed a basket of flavored teas and a small pot of water on the table. Steam rose from the pot, swirling like mist.

Jenny glanced out the window again, lured by the magical scene. A dreamlike trance came over her. "The flowers are beautiful, aren't they?" she asked, watching the ballerinas dance.

"Yes." Daisy shifted her focus. "Sometimes I walk through the garden on my break. I could stay there for hours."

They gazed at each other once more, and Jenny's hands began to tremble. Suddenly she could feel the other woman's emotions flowing through her like a waterfall. She could almost hear the prayers Daisy whispered each night, the softly spoken words mingling with tears.

Dear God. How could this be happening? How could she tap into someone else's heart?

"Are you okay?" Jenny managed to ask, still staring at Daisy.

The other woman blinked, and the connection was gone. "Why wouldn't I be?"

"I don't know. You seemed lost for a minute." You seem lost all the time, Jenny thought.

"I'm fine." The waitress smiled, but the strain around her mouth belied her admission. "But it's sweet of you to ask." She paused, her voice struggling for control. "Actually, there are some issues in my life, but they're nothing I can't handle. Please don't worry about me."

"As long as you're all right."

"I am." She reached for Jenny's hand and gave it a squeeze. "I'm not trying to push you away, but this is complicated. It wouldn't be right to pull you into it."

"If you ever need someone to talk to, you can call me," Jenny said.

"Thank you. But I think we should leave things as they are."

Jenny watched the waitress walk away, wishing she could help, but knowing she couldn't.

Coleman Investigations was located on the third floor of a staunch brick building. The office itself had brass fixtures, sturdy leather chairs and potted plants that grew toward a floor-to-ceiling window.

Hawk sat across from Dusty Randall, a sixty-something private eye, with a down-home accent and an extensive military background.

Randall wore his gray hair cropped short and his boots polished to a slick shine.

Hawk appreciated his no-nonsense attitude. The

consultation was free, and the coffee offered was strong and fresh.

Coleman Investigations was a national business, with associates all over the country.

"A surveillance in Salt Lake City won't be a problem," Randall said. "An activity check would be provided first. Then we'd do our best to obtain and record vital information."

"My main concern is Roy Segal coming to Texas. And I want to know if he appears to be searching for his ex-wife."

"Did Ms. Taylor file a restraining order against him?"

"I don't know. Would it make a difference?"

"Not necessarily. Former intimate-partner stalkers don't usually respond to restraining orders. Was Segal abusive?"

A knot formed in Hawk's chest. "Yes."

"I'm not surprised. Studies show these kind of stalkers were often abusive and controlling during the relationship."

"Jenny is afraid he'll try to kill her."

"Before we go any further, are you aware of the security precautions Ms. Taylor should take?"

"Not really. This is all pretty new to me."

Randall leaned forward. "Does she receive mail at her residence?"

"Yes." Hawk thought about the afternoon she'd fainted, the day he'd received her mail by mistake. "She gets magazine subscriptions and utility bills and things like that at home. I don't think she gets any personal letters. As far as I know, she didn't keep in touch with anyone from Utah. And she doesn't have any family left."

"Tell her to secure a post-office box and use it for all her correspondence. And for places that don't accept a post-office box, change the P.O. box part to apartment and leave the number. Have her put this address on her checks, too. No one needs to know where she lives. She isn't obligated to give out her home address."

Hawk nodded and listened with intent.

"If she doesn't have a cell phone, tell her to get one and keep it with her at all times. She'll need it if her phone lines are ever cut."

As Randall continued to advise Hawk, the threat, the danger of Jenny being hurt became more real.

"She shouldn't accept any packages unless it's something she ordered, and any discarded mail should be destroyed. Now this is a tough one, but I highly recommend it. She needs to tell neighbors and co-workers that her ex-husband has stalked her in the past, and he might be looking for her. This way, if he shows up, they'll know who he is and not to divulge any information about her."

Randall tapped his pen and went on, "I also suggest Ms. Taylor join a victim support group. They can provide invaluable resources, as well as support. My secretary can give you a list of organizations."

"Is it possible to keep Segal under constant surveillance?" Hawk asked.

"We can record his public activity, where he goes, who he talks to. But you have to understand that we can't place cameras or recording devices inside his home or office."

"Can you check into his past activity? Find out if he's been questioning Jenny's old acquaintances about her whereabouts?"

"Yes."

"What kind of fee am I looking at?"

Randall quoted a rate, and Hawk realized he wouldn't be able to afford an extensive investigation. All he could afford were weekly reports that indicated whether or not Roy was still in Salt Lake City.

And that left time in between, time for Roy's activities to go unrecorded, time for him to find his way to Mission Creek without being seen.

Damn it, Hawk thought. Suddenly he wished he had access to the Wainwright fortune. His father was a wealthy man. Archy had plenty of money, but that didn't do Hawk any good. An inheritance wasn't going to magically appear.

"I'm on a limited budget, but this is important. I don't want Segal slipping into Texas without me knowing it."

"We'll work within your budget, and we'll break up the surveillance into smaller sessions. We're more likely to provide useful coverage that way."

Hawk gave Randall the names and numbers of Jenny's old acquaintances and told Randall everything he knew about Roy.

Thirty minutes later their meeting ended.

"Be sure to see my secretary for the list of support groups," the other man said after they shook hands.

"I will." Hawk went to the reception desk, obtained the information, then headed to the parking lot.

He sat in his truck and scanned a pamphlet on domestic violence, and when he came across the term *Battered Woman's Syndrome,* he read the material carefully.

He leaned back against the seat and closed his eyes, conjuring up an image of the gentle woman he'd come to care about. According to this literature, Jenny fit the profile.

She needed a support group, he thought. And she needed a psychologist or counselor to help her cope with her emotions.

Hawk could try to protect her from Roy, but he couldn't protect her from the pain she'd already suffered.

Eight

"I'm so glad you're home," Hawk said as Jenny answered her door.

"My meeting at the club didn't last very long. I've been here for hours."

She looked soft and girlish, and he had the urge to take her in his arms and never let go.

But he schooled his emotions, instead. If he held her, he would want to kiss her, cover her mouth and make her part of him.

Yet he knew that wouldn't protect her. He couldn't let her burrow inside him, like a turtle hiding in its shell. He couldn't shield her from reality.

He gestured to the swing, inviting her to join him. "The P.I. had a lot to say, and I'd like to discuss it with you."

She came out to the porch, and they sat side by side.

He studied the yard for a moment, attempting to take solace from the earth. The afternoon sun shone through the trees, making shadows on the lawn.

Damn it. Why couldn't he let her share his soul? Why couldn't he undo what Roy had done?

"Hawk?"

She said his name, and he turned to look at her. Beautiful, delicate Jenny. She needed more than he could give her.

"What did the P.I. say?"

"First of all, there are some safety precautions you should take." He repeated the bit about the post-office box and offered to take her to get one later that day.

"I didn't leave a forwarding address when I moved, so I didn't think a P.O. box was necessary."

"Apparently it is. And you should have a cell phone." He reached into his pocket. "You can use mine for now. You're supposed to keep it with you at all times, even in your house, in case your phone lines are cut." He made a mental note to give her the charger. "This is important, Jenny."

Silent, she took his cell and placed it on her lap.

He wished he could smooth a hand down her hair. But touching her, he'd already determined, wasn't what this meeting was about.

"I hired Coleman Investigations," he said. "But it isn't possible to keep Roy under constant surveillance. The best we can hope for is knowing his whereabouts, making sure he isn't on his way to Texas."

"Thank you. What you're doing for me means so much."

But it wasn't enough, he thought. Not nearly enough. "Did you file a restraining order against Roy?"

She shook her head. "I got a temporary one, but I never followed through on the permanent order."

"Why not?"

"Because it meant facing Roy in court, and I couldn't cope with that. When he was served with the temporary order, he called me and said some things that scared me. He was so angry. I didn't see how a piece of paper was going to protect me." Now she clutched the cell phone in her hand, her knuckles turning white.

"What did he say to you?"

"He mentioned a woman who had been murdered by her estranged husband. He claimed this man had knifed the restraining order to her chest."

Hawk felt a line of sweat run down his back, chilling him.

"I dropped the charges," she said.

"It's okay, honey. I understand why you did." He wanted to rip Roy Segal apart limb by limb.

She rocked the swing, and he imagined her alone in Salt Lake City, waiting for evil to strike. "You're going to have to tell neighbors and co-workers about Roy. They need to be aware of how dangerous he is. If you explain the situation to Mrs. Pritchett, she'll be on the lookout for him. Hell, it will probably give the old busybody something to do. And the folks at the country club need to know, too."

When stubborn blue eyes locked on to his, Hawk knew he was in for a fight. "Damn it, woman. You have to. This isn't negotiable."

"The hell it isn't." She made a sound of frustration. "I don't want people knowing. Can you imagine what that would do to my career? My reputation? I've worked hard to establish myself in Mission Creek."

He swore beneath his breath. "Your reputation? People are already talking about you. They think you're sleeping with me."

"That's different. Having an affair doesn't make me seem weak. But being stalked by an abusive ex-husband will turn me into a victim. That's all people will see when they look at me."

"This could save your life, Jenny."

"Or it could destroy it. I have to live in this town. I have to work here. I'm not going to shame myself by telling people about my past."

"I'll tell them. I'll explain—"

"No!" she all but shouted at him.

"Then get some help, damn it." He snapped the list of support groups from his back pocket and thrust it at her. If he couldn't talk some sense into her, maybe someone else could.

"What's this?" She scanned the heading and shoved the paper back at him. "I don't need to sit around and talk about what Roy did to me. I got away from him." When Hank refused to take the list back, she dropped it onto his lap. "And do you know how I got away?"

Hawk shook his head, his mouth set in a grim line. She was acting braver than she was, he was certain, feigning a confidence she didn't have.

"I outsmarted Roy. I made plans to escape. I accepted the job in Mission Creek and waited for the right moment to leave. When Roy wasn't threatening me, he was apologizing, sending flowers and plants and stuffed animals." She made a bitter face, letting Hawk know the gifts had appalled her. "But I figured it would be easier to slip away when he was in one of his courting moods. He didn't watch me so closely then."

"Did you flee in the middle of the night?"

"Yes. I was scared, but I did what I had to do to survive. I'm not a victim anymore."

But she is, Hawk thought. She has nightmares about Roy, yet she refuses to follow all of the safety precautions. "It wouldn't hurt to talk to someone,

Jenny. A therapist. A support group. You've been through a hell of an ordeal.''

"I'm healing on my own. *Our* relationship is proof of that."

Why? he wondered. Because she was giving herself time to adjust to him? To kiss him? To touch him?

He searched her gaze. "What are you hiding? Why are you so afraid of going to a support group? What do you think they're going to uncover?"

"Nothing," she snapped.

"You're lying, Jenny. I can see it on your face. In your gestures." In the clouds in her eyes, the nervous flutter of her hands.

"Stop pressuring me." She jammed the phone back into his shirt pocket, more or less telling him to go to hell.

He held her riled gaze. "Did I hit a nerve?"

"You're trying to take over my life."

"I'm trying to be a friend," he countered.

"Well, stop trying so damn hard."

Before he could respond, she rushed into her house and slammed the door, locking away tears and secrets she refused to reveal.

He cursed. And then prayed he hadn't lost her.

All that day and into the evening, between tearful bursts of emotion, Jenny had paced, stared blankly at the walls or curled up in a fetal position on the floor.

And now she sat on the edge of her bed, filled with remorse. Hawk didn't deserve her wrath. He didn't deserve to be punished for something Roy had done.

She owed him an apology. And an explanation.

But how she could look him in the eye and admit

the truth? The stomach-clenching, humiliating, shame-ridden truth?

She glanced at herself in the mirrored closet doors. An ebony nightgown poured over her body like a veil, making her skin seem paler, her hair a lighter shade of blond. The translucent circles under her eyes gave her a haunted, tortured quality.

No matter how painful the truth was, she had to tell Hawk. If she didn't, her secret would destroy the bridge they'd been building, the friendship they'd both come to rely on.

But how should she say it? What words should she use? And where should she direct her gaze?

Admitting what Roy had done to her was bad enough, but looking at Hawk during this new admission would kill her. She couldn't bear to see his revulsion, the twist of his features, the pity in his eyes.

Then call him, a small voice in her head said. Use the phone. Let it be your shield.

Still sitting on the edge of her bed, Jenny lifted the receiver and dialed his number, her heart vibrating with every peal.

"Hello?" he answered on the seventh ring, his voice a rough bass.

She looked at the clock, suddenly worried she'd roused him from much-needed sleep. "Did I wake you?" she asked, regretting the call.

"Jenny? No, I was in the shower. Are you okay, honey?"

"Yes, I'm fine." She pictured him rugged and wet, a towel wrapped around his waist, his shampoo-scented hair dripping water down his back.

She climbed under the covers, wishing she could

put her head on his shoulder and absorb the moisture with her cheek. "I'm sorry I yelled at you, Hawk."

"That's all right. Everyone is entitled to a mood swing now and then."

He paused, and she wondered if he was adjusting his towel, if the terry cloth cover had slipped lower.

"I shouldn't have pressured you," he said.

"I really don't want to go to a support group." She didn't want to talk to strangers about her past. And she didn't want to spend several hours a week listening to strangers talk about their experiences. She couldn't bear to subject herself to reminders of what she'd been through. What if some of the other women were still suffering from abuse? Their bruises would slam straight into her soul, like the swift, brutal fists that had created them.

"Maybe you'll change your mind someday, Jenny. Maybe it will get easier as time goes on."

She didn't respond. Instead, she hugged a pillow to her chest.

Silence stilled the air, drawing scents and images closer. Cinnamon-spiced potpourri filled her nostrils as silver-laced moonbeams flirted with the blinds, creating jagged shadows on an opposing wall.

"Jenny?" Hawk asked. "Are you still there?"

"Yes." Her voice came out in a whisper. "There's something I need to tell you."

"I'm listening."

She stared at the slashing shadows on the wall. "I'm so ashamed of what I let Roy do."

"Don't you dare blame yourself for his abuse. You're not responsible for his actions. He didn't beat you because you provoked him."

She hugged the pillow more tightly. "I'm not talk-

ing about the times he hit me. I'm talking about the
times I gave in to his demands so he wouldn't beat
me.''

"It's only natural to try to protect yourself. Whatever you did to fend him off was part of your survival.''

"No, it wasn't.'' It was part of her destruction. Her
humiliation and guilt. "I let him have sex with me,
even after I knew I was going to leave him.'' She
pictured herself, numb and unresponsive as Roy
pounded his body into hers. "The day I lost the baby,
I made up my mind to leave him, but I didn't move
out right away. I meant to, but when my mother died,
I fell apart. There was so much to cope with.'' So
much emptiness, so much pain. "I wasn't strong
enough to tell Roy that I wanted a divorce. I was
afraid of how he would react. So I gave myself a little
time, and I avoided him the best I could.''

Hawk didn't respond, so she continued, rocking
herself for comfort, "Roy was actually being nice. He
felt guilty about the baby and knew I was grieving
for my mother. He didn't question why I was so distant with him. He just kept trying to make it up to
me.''

She squeezed her eyes shut, the memory rising like
bile. "But one night he approached me. It had been
three weeks since the miscarriage, and he wanted to
have sex. I told him it was too soon. It was the only
excuse I could think of, but he didn't buy it.''

She heard Hawk's sharp intake of breath, but she
went on before he could interrupt. "I tried to reason
with him and I kept saying no, but he pushed me onto
the bed. I started to fight him off, but when I saw the
rage in his eyes, I gave in. I stopped fighting.''

"He raped you, Jenny." The tone in Hawk's voice rasped through the receiver, chilling the air. "That low-life, scum-sucking son of a bitch raped you."

"I gave in."

"What were you supposed to do? Keep fighting him off?"

"Yes."

"He would have raped you, anyway. And he would have beat you while he was doing it."

"I know. But afterward my weakness shamed me. I should have scratched his eyes out. I should have fumed and screamed and kicked. But I gave up. I just stared at the ceiling and tried to pretend I was somewhere else. I acted like a coward."

"No, you didn't," he said gently. "Psychologists call it the 'fight or flight' response. Since you couldn't escape physically, you disassociated yourself from what was happening. That's nothing to be ashamed of."

"Where did you learn that?"

"From a pamphlet on domestic violence."

Oh, God, she thought. He'd been reading about abused women, trying to understand her, trying to make sense of her emotions. She didn't know whether to cringe or cry.

"In the old Apache way, rape was avenged by the family of the woman who'd been wronged," he said. "Do you want me to be your family? I'd be glad to make Roy pay for what he did. I can think of a thousand ways to torture him."

Tears gathered in her eyes, and she sniffed into the phone. "Thank you for caring, Hawk." And for reading that disturbing pamphlet, she added mentally. For offering to be her family.

"Are you crying?"

She sniffed again. "Sort of. Not really."

"Yes, you are. Do you want me to come over? I can bunk on your couch. Or I can…"

"What?" she asked when his words died.

"Hold you while you sleep."

She looked at her bed and imagined him in it, his skin warm and bronzed, his arms strong and solid. The sheets and pillow shams were too frilly for him, too flowery and girlish, but she knew his masculinity wouldn't be diminished by rosebuds and lace.

"I can bring Muddy," he said. "He can be our chaperon."

Jenny laughed through her tears. "I'll unlock the back door. For both of you."

"All right." She heard a smile in his voice. "But I still have to get dressed."

She refused to picture him removing the towel. "What do you sleep in?"

When he didn't answer, she said, "Hawk?"

"Umm—" he paused "—you don't really want to know, do you?"

Her face went hot. He slept naked.

"But I'll wear some sweats tonight," he told her. "Or shorts or something. Or maybe I'll just put on a pair of jeans. That would probably be best."

She cursed herself for asking in the first place. "That's up to you."

"Are you wearing one of those pretty night-gowns?"

Her face went hot again. "It's black." Like the night, like his hair. If they kept this conversation going, her nerves were going to burst right out of her skin.

"Muddy's wearing a new collar," Hawk said, and Jenny knew he was hoping to ease the sudden tension. "Leather with those little silver spikes."

She laughed. "Just tell him to get his butt over here."

"Yes, ma'am. We'll see you in a few."

After they hung up, Jenny went to the back door and unlocked it, then waited for Hawk to arrive.

God help her, she was nervous again, worried about being in the same bed with him. What if he got aroused? What if he—

The door opened, and Muddy, brimming with youth and canine clumsiness, squeezed through the opening and slid onto the kitchen floor.

The door opened farther, and Jenny saw Hawk's moccasin-covered feet. Rather than lift her gaze, she kept it fixed on the dog.

Muddy ran to her, eager to be petted. She knelt to oblige and noticed the spiked collar.

"I thought you were kidding." She glanced up at Hawk and felt the earth tilt on its axis.

His hair twined over his shoulders and down his naked chest like midnight vines, inviting his nipples to peek through the dark mass. A pair of old, frayed Wranglers with holes in both knees rode low on his hips.

She rose, leaving the puppy dancing around her feet.

"Kidding about what?" Hawk asked, his eyes connecting with hers.

"Muddy's collar."

"I bought it yesterday."

And tonight he stood in her kitchen waiting for her to lead him to her bed.

"Should w-we...?" she stammered.

"Lie down?" he finished.

Jenny nodded and Hawk moved closer.

"Are you nervous, honey?"

"Yes."

"About us?"

"Yes," she said again.

"Don't be."

He slipped his arms around her and drew her to his chest. When he stroked her hair, she closed her eyes. Somehow he'd captured the scent of the night, the fragrance of the wind and the trees and the grass. She could smell the elements clinging to his skin.

"I'm just here to hold you," he said. "To protect you."

His declaration conveyed strength and sincerity. She opened her eyes and looked up at him. "Are you my warrior, Hawk?"

"I am if that's what you want me to be. I'd do anything to keep you safe." He picked her up and carried her down the hall.

It was a move she hadn't expected, a move that made her feel soft and secure, snug within his power.

"You weigh barely more than a whisper," he said.

Because, she thought, her bones had turned as light as feathers.

Muddy raced past, and when they entered Jenny's room, the puppy waited for them on the bed, reigning over the rosebuds and lace with an impatient swish of his tail.

"Looks like our chaperon is taking his job seriously," Hawk said as he placed her next to the dog.

The puppy licked her face, shocking her bones

back into their regular form. His nose was cold; his canine kisses sloppy and wet.

She laughed and ruffled his floppy ears.

Hawk removed his moccasins and smiled at her.

Jenny returned his smile. This feeling of family was just what she needed. Hawk had chased away her tears, the isolation and nightmare-induced fear that came with sleeping alone.

They climbed under the covers, and he fitted her against him, with her head resting on his shoulder. The embrace was strong yet gentle, and she knew he hoped to soothe her, to help her recover from the horror of what Roy had done.

Hawk's actions, she thought as she snuggled closer, spoke of friendship and trust. Tonight held nothing but the promise of a protective slumber.

"Do you want me to turn off the light?" he asked.

"Just dim it," she responded, not wanting to lose sight of him.

"No problem." He reached over to turn down the three-way bulb.

The quiet calmed Muddy, and he found a cozy spot next to Jenny, pressing his little body against her hip.

Jenny heard a soft tap-tapping at the window and realized it had begun to rain. The TV weatherman had predicted a light shower, but she'd forgotten about the report until now.

Muddy lifted his head and perked his ears, and Jenny assumed this was the dog's first experience with the sound of rain. Tomorrow there would be fresh mud for him to explore.

"This is a female rain," Hawk said.

"What do you mean?"

"To the Chiricahua, a heavy, driving rain is male, but a light one is female."

He shifted so they lay face-to-face, their heads resting on the same pillow. His eyes, she noticed, glowed in the night-shrouded room, his pupils catching a spark from the lamp.

"Do you know why it rains?" he asked.

"Vapors in the atmosphere, I think." She couldn't recall the exact science, the information she'd been taught in elementary school. And she'd never analyzed rain as an adult.

"In my culture a Water Being is responsible for rain," he told her. "He Who Controls Water lives above, wearing a shirt of colored clouds." Hawk gestured with his hands. "They say he guards the water gate. He lets it flow or he shuts it off. Like a faucet, I suppose. If you know his song, you can sing to him and he'll make it rain."

"Do you think someone sang to him tonight?" she asked, fascinated by the supernatural images of his world.

"Maybe."

"What other beings are associated with the Apache?"

"Ysun is the supreme being, the Life Giver. White Painted Woman, an important female deity, has existed from the beginning. Her son is Child of Water." He paused to adjust the blanket, giving Muddy an excuse to wiggle before settling down again with a big, puppy yawn. "After a child takes his or her first steps, a ceremony is held, and the power comes from Child of Water, because he went through this ceremony when he learned to walk."

"Did your mom have a ceremony for you?" She

pictured him, a little Apache boy with dark eyes and flyaway hair, taking his first steps.

He nodded. "I don't remember it of course, but she told me about it. A shaman was called, and he directed my mom to make me a buckskin outfit, decorated with crescents, stars and crosses. My grandmother helped, and on the day of the ceremony they prepared a feast for the guests. But before anyone could eat, prayers were said and songs were sung. My moccasins were marked with sacred pollen, and I was encouraged to walk. The guests feasted all day, and later that night, I was lifted toward the moon so I would grow tall."

"That sounds like a beautiful ceremony." And now she knew how he had acquired his height.

"Every child should touch the moon," he said. "And wear stars on their clothes."

They both fell silent after that, and he put his arms around her.

Jenny melted against him, absorbing his warmth. She'd cried half the day, but tonight she was safe in Hawk's arms, with a female rain tapping softly on the window. She put her head against his heart and listened to the strong, steady beats.

A moment later she closed her eyes and slept.

Nine

Hawk dreamed he was in an unfamiliar bed, with the warm, sensual sensation of a woman's body next to his, their legs entwined.

Half-asleep and fully aroused, he reached for her, bringing her closer. She felt soft, silky—a fantasy his mind had conjured. Yet as he held her, she became more real.

Flesh and bone. Too solid to be a dream.

With sudden awareness he opened his eyes.

And saw Jenny staring back at him.

She looked like a fairy-tale princess, her gold-streaked hair catching the morning light, her lashes fluttering, her skin a pale wash of ivory.

Beautiful. Vulnerable. And oh, so real.

Did she notice? Did she feel the bulge beneath his zipper?

This wasn't supposed to happen, damn it. He wasn't supposed to have these urges. Not now. Not while he was consoling her from a nightmarish past.

"We're all tangled up," he said.

Her cheeks flushed. "It must have happened when we were asleep."

"Yeah." Feeling guilty, he shifted his hips and tried to untangle the blanket.

Jenny moved, too, but her nightgown started to bunch and she froze.

"Sorry." He did his damnedest to free himself without causing her distress.

Muddy jumped into the thick of it, and all was lost. The puppy grabbed hold of Hawk's pant leg and yanked the fabric, trying to initiate a game of tug-of-war.

Jenny watched the exchange, and then burst out laughing.

Hawk should have laughed, too. But he was too embarrassed to do anything but battle with Muddy over the right to take his leg back.

"No!" he told the puppy. "No!"

The dog refused to back down. He snarled and tugged, his teeth clamped tight.

"You two make quite a pair," Jenny said, her eyes sparkling with mirth.

"Oh, yeah? Well, I don't see you faring much better."

The hem of her skewed nightgown was still trapped beneath his other leg, the one Muddy wasn't attacking.

She tried to pull it out from under him, but Hawk decided not to let her off the hook. He rolled over, using his weight to keep her garment in place.

"You're doing that on purpose."

"Am I?" He shot her a smug grin. "I guess that will teach you to laugh at a grown man being ambushed by a puppy."

"Oh, really?"

She grabbed the nearest pillow and smacked him over the head with it.

And that was all it took.

They got into a knockdown, drag-out fight. But they didn't contain their pillow mischief to the bed.

They raced through the house like a couple of kids, Muddy chasing after them with glee.

Jenny squealed as Hawk rounded a corner, then took the girl's way out and locked herself in the bathroom.

"That's cheating!" he yelled through the door.

"So sue me."

He heard her breathless laughter and realized he'd never had so much fun.

Muddy twirled in the hall and barked at him. *Are you going to let her get away with that?* he seemed to be saying.

"Hell, no," Hawk responded.

The dog barked again. *Then what are you gonna do?*

"Come with me and I'll show you."

The puppy followed him into the kitchen, where Hawk slit one side of the pillow. "It's down," he told the dog. "Filled with feathers," he explained, giving one to Muddy to sniff.

Woof. Woof. A curious tilt of the head. *It smells expensive.*

"I'll buy her a new one." He tucked the fluffy weapon under his arm. "Now let's take our revenge."

They trotted into the hall, man and dog, grinning foolishly at each other.

"Jenny?" Hawk called.

"What?" came the suspicious reply.

"I can't stay any longer. I have an appointment at eight. And I still have to go home and get dressed."

"You didn't say anything about an appointment last night."

"I didn't think of it," he told her.

"Are you leaving right now?" she asked.

"Yes."

"This isn't some sort of trick?"

"No." He gestured for Muddy to keep his mouth shut. The dog looked as if he might snicker.

"Are you sure?"

"Yes."

"If you're lying—"

"I'm not."

She opened the door a crack, and he held out his empty hands. "See?" He'd stashed the pillow just a few feet away.

She stepped out of the bathroom, and when she did, he moved like lightning. He grabbed the pillow and pelted her with it, sending a cloud of feathers flying.

She let out another one of those girlish squeals and took off running, Muddy and Hawk right on her heels.

And finally, when the last feather was expelled, they collapsed on the living-room floor and laughed until their sides ached.

Muddy rolled around in the mess, sniffing and sneezing. Hawk sat up and studied Jenny. Tufts of white clung to her hair and settled on her shoulders, making her look like the angel she was.

She met his gaze, and the moment turned soft and quiet.

"We could be in heaven," she said, as feathers drifted around them like snowflakes. Capturing one in her palm, she blew it toward him like a kiss.

He smiled and caught it with his heart.

"I forgot to tell you what happened yesterday." She scooted onto the couch, taking her angel wings with her. Turning, she lifted a roll-up blind on the window behind, allowing light to seep through a sheer lace curtain. "I connected with someone, the way you connected with me."

"What do you mean?" He remained on the floor, awed by her beauty.

"Do you know who Daisy Parker is?" she asked.

He shook his head.

"She's a waitress at the country club. And from the day I first met her, I sensed something sad about her. But yesterday I almost read her mind." Jenny smoothed her nightgown, and the ebony silk molded to her body. "It was so strange, Hawk. I actually felt her emotions."

"The way I felt yours on the night I had that dream."

She nodded. "I was sitting in the Yellow Rose Café, staring out the window at the garden. And then everything turned sort of mystical. A white bird landed on a bench, and the flowers started to sway."

He moved a little closer, and she continued, explaining what had transpired between her and Daisy. "It was the strangest moment of my life. For an instant in time, I could feel the tears she'd cried, like a waterfall rushing through me."

"It was the dove," Hawk said.

"What dove? You mean the white bird?"

He gazed at her, this beautiful, blue-eyed woman dusted with feathers. "The dove is your messenger, Jenny. It's part of your spirit."

"But I don't know anything about doves. I can't even be sure that's the kind of bird it was. Besides, white doves are rare, aren't they?"

"It might have been bred for ceremonies."

"Like the ones released at weddings?"

He nodded.

"And it just happened to take a little detour to visit me?"

He nodded again, and then smiled at her perplexed expression. "You're going to see it again, Jenny. It will appear another day."

Her breath caught. "How do you know that?"

"I just do." He also knew that doves mated for life. Which meant Jenny's spirit guide probably had a partner, a lover that might appear, as well.

"What does all of this have to do with Daisy?" she asked.

"I'm not sure. But eventually you'll find out. The dove will show you."

"I think this happened because of you," she said. "You brought magic into my life. Visions and dreams and ceremonial doves."

Touched by her words, he watched the morning sun illuminate her in a hazy glow. "Will you go on a date with me?" he asked. "Will you let me take you out tonight?"

"Yes," she responded without hesitation.

They smiled at each other and then began to clean up the feathers.

Maybe this was heaven. Or a tiny slice of it.

Daisy paced her apartment. She lived in a place she rented on a month-by-month basis. And although it came nicely furnished, it would never be home.

This was hell, she thought. Not the apartment, but the circumstances of her life.

She stopped pacing and looked around. Nothing spoke of her true identity. Her personal belongings were few, essentials that wouldn't link her to Haley Mercado.

"Haley Mercado," she said out loud. Someday she would be able to reclaim her life. Her identity. Her soul.

She had become Daisy Parker a little more than a year ago, just two weeks after Lena was born.

Lena. Her beautiful daughter. Her baby girl.

Daisy's heart contracted, and she said a quiet prayer for Lena. She prayed for her kidnapped child every night, asking God to keep Lena safe.

She moved to the window and gazed out, the events of Haley's life spinning before her mind's eye.

She had been born into the Texas mob, but her greatest desire was to escape. Haley loved her parents and her brother, but she'd decided that staging her own death was the only way to break free.

And that was what she had done.

With the help of a trusted friend, Haley Mercado had drowned in a boating accident.

Daisy sank onto the couch and touched her altered face. After her supposed drowning, she'd moved to London, England, where she'd undergone plastic surgery—her classic Italian features were modified to look more Anglo—and bleached her hair, becoming someone new.

But two years ago she'd come back to Mission Creek when she'd heard that her mother had been severely beaten and lay ill in the hospital because her father had refused to carry out an order. So Haley, disguised as a nun, had slipped into the hospital room to comfort her mother.

Later that night Haley had never felt more alone. Needing a drink, she'd gone to the Saddlebag, a local bar, where she'd come across someone from her past, a man who had no way of recognizing her. A man she'd always wanted.

She'd never given him her name, but they'd ended up in each other's arms, steeped in one glorious night of passion.

And when Haley returned to London, she'd discovered she was pregnant with his child.

And now here she was, more than a year later, helping the FBI take down the Texas mob. The feds had promised to give her father and brother immunity, as well as help Haley reclaim her old life.

She had to do this, for herself and her family. Her mother had eventually been murdered, and Haley knew the violence wouldn't end until her enemies were destroyed.

But what good was resuming her old life without Lena? As tears flooded her eyes, Haley/Daisy rocked herself in shallow comfort.

Nothing mattered but her daughter, the beautiful little girl with the sweet smile and loving arms.

Oh, God. The urge to pace came over her again, and she stalked the room with nervous energy.

She didn't want to stay home, isolated and alone. She wanted…

What? Lena's father to hold her? To comfort her?

She couldn't let that happen. She couldn't tell him who she was. She'd tried to leave Lena in his care, certain the child would be safe with him, but her plan had backfired. He hadn't gotten to know their daughter. Lena had been kidnapped, instead.

And now Daisy longed to be in his arms, longed

to put her head on his shoulder and draw strength from the warmth of his body.

She closed her eyes and thought about the night she'd met him at the Saddlebag, the starlit evening they'd sat by the fireplace and listened to country ballads fill the air.

In a sweet, reminiscent moment, she let the flames console her.

And then she opened her eyes and fell into the deep, dark pit of reality.

Reliving that wondrous night wouldn't end the pain she was in now.

It was a wondrous night, Jenny thought. Stars winked in the sky like sapphires reflecting a shimmer of blue.

Hawk parked his truck, and they climbed out and walked to the entrance of the bar. The Saddlebag was housed in a plain-looking building, with a wooden sign announcing its name.

Hawk's hand brushed Jenny's, and she turned to give him a shy smile. They'd slept in the same bed, but this was their first date. And somehow it seemed more intimate.

The interior of the Saddlebag was dim, Jenny noticed, with a large bar and a grouping of about ten or fifteen tables. A pool table, a dartboard and lone pinball machine dominated the rear, and a tiny dance floor had been crowded into a cozy spot. But the true charm, she thought, was the fireplace, set amid a few plush chairs and cushioned couches.

"Can we sit by the fire?" she asked. The ground

outside was still damp from the day's rain, and a fire-place seemed like the perfect setting.

"Sure. You get comfortable, and I'll order our drinks." He paused to adjust his hat, a charcoal Stetson that complemented the shock of black hair streaming over his shoulders. "What do you want, honey?"

You, she thought suddenly. I want you.

"White wine is fine."

"You got it."

She watched him head to the bar, her pulse jittery.

Hawk Wainwright, she thought. Her neighbor, her friend, her proud, protective warrior. She couldn't help but want him.

Before her knees gave way, she took a seat on the sofa closest to the fireplace. The Saddlebag wasn't busy, and she assumed the patrons who dotted the bar considered it their local watering hole on a Thursday night.

Hawk returned with a glass of chardonnay for her and a bottle of beer for himself. He sat next to her, and they remained quiet for a short time.

Jenny could hear a clacking sound coming from the pool table where two men played a challenging game. The pinball machine stood silent, no whistles, bobs or bells signaling its use.

"I like this place," she said finally. The walls held a collection of Texas memorabilia. It reminded her of the changes in her life, of the newness she'd found in Mission Creek.

"I like it, too. I come here once in a while, but I've never sat by the fire."

"Where do you usually sit?"

He motioned with his beer. "At the bar."

Like the rest of the loners, Jenny thought. She sipped her wine and felt it warm her blood.

Or maybe it was Hawk warming her blood. The flames cast a flickering glow over his skin, highlighting the planes and angles of his face. The black talons she'd become accustomed to danced in his ears. She doubted that he ever removed them. She already knew he wore them to bed.

"Where should we have dinner?" he asked, interrupting her thoughts.

She couldn't focus beyond the heat flowing through her veins. "I don't know."

He took a pull of his beer. "I want you to decide, Jenny."

Taking a deep breath, she labored over a decision, and when she came up with an idea, she hoped he wouldn't think it was foolish. "I've always wanted to eat at one of those fifties-type drive-ins. There's one in this tiny town called Sandy Ville, about thirty miles off the old road. They bring your food to the car." She toyed with her wineglass, twisting the stem. "I saw it when I first came to Texas. I took a wrong turn and ended up in Sandy Ville."

A grin split Hawk's face. "You want to eat in the truck?"

She nodded. "Like they did in the fifties. Life seemed so simple then. So innocent." And tonight she wanted to be part of that innocence.

"Then let's do this right," he said. "Let's see if the jukebox has any fifties tunes."

He took her hand and led her to the old-fashioned record machine.

Early rock and roll was out of the question, but the jukebox offered plenty of vintage country.

They chose a trio of Buck Owens's older hits, along with a Hank Williams number that crooned about a cheating heart.

When the first song started, Hawk looked into her eyes. "Will you dance with me?" he asked.

She nodded, and they walked onto the tiny dance floor. They were the only couple swaying to the music, but Jenny didn't mind. She put her head on Hawk's shoulder and let the moment carry her away.

The road to Sandy Ville was old and bumpy, but Hawk's truck took the terrain with ease.

Jenny directed him to the drive-in eatery, and he parked in a fairly quiet spot.

"So what do you think?" she asked.

"It definitely has charm." A simple building and a basic burgers-and-fries menu presented vestiges of the past without being trendy. But then, a town like Sandy Ville didn't set trends. Hawk suspected the Coupe de Ville Diner, with its neon sign and eat-in-your-car convenience, was the brainchild of a local proprietor missing his youth.

A teenage carhop wearing jeans and a Cadillac T-shirt took their order and went back to the diner.

"It's a beautiful night," Jenny said.

Hawk glanced out the windshield at the vast, star-scattered night sky.

"It is pretty," he agreed.

She turned to smile at him, and he reached for her hand. She looked fresh and appealing in her denim dress, buttoned from collar to hem, and with her hair framing her face in loose waves. Even in the dim light, her eyes shone bright and blue.

She leaned toward him, and he knew she was giving him permission to kiss her. Their lips brushed tenderly, as light as a whisper, as soft and mouthwatering as cotton candy on a summer day.

Needing more, Hawk intensified the kiss. He cupped her face and teased her lips with his tongue. Her lips parted eagerly.

"Your order's ready."

The carhop's voice jarred them apart.

Hawk nearly bruised his elbow on the steering wheel, and Jenny started fussing with her dress as if she needed something to do.

He turned to the teenager and the girl rolled her eyes, telling them she thought he was a bit too old to be seducing his date at a drive-in.

Hawk accepted the food and gave the girl a tip to get rid of her. He wasn't that old, was he?

He handed Jenny her meal, and they looked at each other awkwardly.

Caught in a wave of silence, they focused on their food. Hawk grabbed a handful of fries and wondered what he should say to ease the tension.

She unwrapped her cheeseburger, then placed a straw in her shake.

They'd slept in the same bed, he thought. So how could one interrupted kiss make them so damn uncomfortable?

Because they were hungry for each other. So damn hungry.

He watched her suck on the straw and felt his groin tighten.

"Is that good?" he asked.

She nodded. "It's really thick. Do you want a taste?"

"Sure." He put his mouth where hers had been and took a long, slow drink. The vanilla milkshake affected him like a cool, creamy aphrodisiac. "Do you want to taste my soda? It's cherry."

"Okay."

She sipped from his straw, and he imagined the sweet, syrupy liquid sliding down her throat.

Was this innocence or insanity? he wondered.

Jenny returned his soda, and he returned the vanilla shake. They were both adults, but they couldn't summon the strength to say what was on their minds.

Kissing, touching, making love.

A small breeze blew through Hawk's window, carrying scents from the night.

"Are you cold?" he asked.

"No. I'm actually warm."

"Yeah, me, too." But desire heated a person's blood, he thought.

When another awkward lull stretched between them, Jenny said, "Did you read your place mat?"

He glanced at the disposable carton holding his food. He'd squirted ketchup all over the place mat. "No. What does it say?"

"That drive-in theaters were inspired by drive-in restaurants."

"Really?" He dipped a fry into his mess of ketchup. "I thought it was the other way around."

"Nope. According to this, the first drive-in theater opened in Camden, New Jersey, in 1933."

"What about the first drive-in diner?"

"It doesn't say. But it must have been established before then." She glanced at her place mat. "The drive-in heyday was in the fifties, though, so that's why most people associate places like this with that era." She smiled a little. "Me included."

Her smile made him warmer than he already was. He wanted to kiss that curved mouth, taste her with his tongue. But he went after his burger, instead.

She followed suit, and they watched each other eat, longing to sate a craving that had nothing to do with food.

Ten

An hour later Jenny and Hawk stood on her porch. The evening was over, and she contemplated what to say.

I want you, but I'm still nervous. When you touch me, my knees go weak. I've never needed a man the way I need you.

"Thank you," she heard herself say, instead. "I had a wonderful time."

"Me, too," he responded quietly.

The security light flooded him with an amber glow. Although his hat shaded his face, gold streaks slashed his clothes, catching the pearl snaps on his shirt.

She wondered if he was thinking about their unfinished kiss. Jenny still tingled from the temptation of his tongue.

Unable to help herself, she reached up to skim his cheek with her fingers.

"Hawk."

"Jenny."

He put his arms around her, then slid his hands to the curve of her spine, drawing her closer. So close she could feel his body beckoning hers.

Their mouths came together then, rekindling the kiss they'd lost.

He moaned his pleasure, and somewhere in the

back of her mind, she felt the rush of wings, the soaring, gliding motion of being lifted into the air.

She grasped his shoulders and held on. And as his tongue dived for hers, the dance intensified. They kissed, over and over, taking and giving, seeking and finding.

And then she felt the hardness, the press of his fly against her stomach. When he adjusted their bodies so his arousal teased the warmth spreading between her legs, Jenny gasped.

She got a mental image of a courtship flight, of a male bird circling the female, then swooping down with incredible speed.

Swooping…swooping…swooping…

Suddenly Hawk broke the connection and stepped back, his breathing labored.

Jenny teetered, stars spinning like pinwheels around her in the sky.

"Are you okay?" he asked.

She managed a shaky nod.

He searched her gaze, and for the longest time they just stood on the porch, staring at each other.

"Tell me what to do," he said finally. "Tell me if I should go home alone or take you with me."

"I'm still nervous," she admitted.

"Then maybe we shouldn't do this. Not now."

But she wanted to. She wanted to continue the courtship flight. The mating between the hawk and the dove.

"I'm confused," she told him. "I never expected to need someone so badly." Yet she liked the rush, the feeling of soaring in the air.

"Me, neither." He made a rough sound, and she

could see the war waging in his eyes. He didn't want to let her go.

"This is crazy." She fell against him, and he stroked her hair.

"The choice is yours, Jenny."

She lifted her head. "Then I choose you." She chose tenderness over trepidation. Arousal over apprehension. Need over nerves.

"I'll be good to you," he whispered, brushing her lips with the taste of his.

"I know," she said against his mouth.

They kissed, softly this time. And then he led her to his house.

He unlocked the front door and they stepped inside.

"I have protection here," he said, explaining why he'd suggested his home, not hers.

Jenny nodded, grateful he'd taken responsibility for such matters. She could barely think beyond the need, beyond the anxious desire that made her heart flutter.

"Muddy's on the patio," he told her. "So we don't have to worry about him bugging us."

"Oh. Okay." She'd forgotten about the puppy, but now she pictured him outside all alone.

"Muddy has lots of toys to play with in his doghouse," Hawk said, as if he'd read her mind.

"Can we bring him in later?" she asked.

"Sure. But for now it's just us."

He smiled at her, and when she smiled back, he swept her up in his arms and carried her down the hall. She clung to his neck and inhaled his scent, the woodsy spice wrapping her in warmth.

Hawk's room reflected the man. A rustic bed draped with a muted Indian blanket gave the Apache cowboy a place to sleep, and a leather shield, decorated with feathers and shimmering beads, added a splash of color.

He set her on her feet, and they stood beside the bed, locked in each other's arms.

"I don't want you to be nervous," he said, removing his hat and placing it on her head with boyish affection.

"Then let me touch you first." She ran her thumb along the waistband of his jeans.

He dropped his arms to his sides, his eyes turning glassy. "I'm yours, Jenny. You can do anything you want."

His surrender gave her power. She untucked his shirt and opened the pearl-covered snaps. With deliberate slowness, she circled one flat brown nipple, then scraped a fingernail down his stomach.

He made an incoherent sound—a low Apache mumble or a rough English curse, she couldn't be sure.

Jenny unbuckled his belt and saw a shiver race through him. And when she unzipped the jeans and slipped her hand inside, she found him hard and thick and generously male. She circled him with her hand and stroked, caressing gently.

Moisture beaded at the tip, and she knew that if she increased the rhythm, she could bring him to a warm, wet, semen-spilling climax.

He covered her mouth and kissed her, and she brought his idle fingers to the top button on her dress, offering to share the power, the need to touch and be touched.

He opened each tiny button and removed her garment with care. As it slid to the hardwood floor, he unhooked her bra and bared her breasts.

He kissed her nipples, and she held him, increasing the sensation. He licked and suckled and drove her to near madness. And then she found herself seated on the edge of his bed, wearing nothing but his hat and her cotton panties.

The wisp of cotton didn't last long. Soon she was naked, with Hawk kneeling between her thighs, the hat threatening to fall off her head as he moved his restless mouth over her.

He dipped his tongue into her navel and slid lower. Then he paused to look up at her, to ask permission.

"Tell me you want this as much as I do."

She peered at him under the brim of his hat, feeling deliciously free and feminine, more sensual than she imagined possible.

"I do," she told him.

"Are you going to watch?" he asked.

Suddenly shy, she nodded, grateful her eyes were shielded.

He sent her a masculine smile and lowered his head, tasting her with his warm, moist tongue.

She bucked on contact and tangled both hands in his hair. He gave her pleasure—pulse pounding, fire-inducing, lust-driven pleasure.

And then she soared into the air, flying into the stillness of the night, chasing mystery and magic and moonbeams.

The hat fell to the floor as she climaxed on a sob, racing through a starlit sky.

When it ended, he coaxed her onto the bed and brought his half-naked body next to hers, which told her the courtship flight, the silk of flesh against flesh, wing against wing, had just began.

*   *   *

Hawk held Jenny, wishing this moment could last forever. She gazed at him through shimmering blue eyes, an angel whose heart beat just for him.

She ran her hands down his back, and when she reached his jeans, he helped her remove them.

The motion was stopped by his boots, and they both laughed. He'd forgotten to remove them.

He kicked them off, and they rolled across the bed, laughing and kissing.

He kept his fingers moving, his hands questing. He touched her everywhere. Soft, smooth flesh, subtle curves, tousled hair. When she arched her back, her nipples brushed his chest, teasing him.

She looked like heaven itself, and she smelled as sweet as spring, tasted better than raspberries dipped in cream.

Like a hungry tom, he took his pleasure—a lick of a delicate shoulder, a nibble of long, pale neck. He'd already tasted her, kissed and laved between her thighs, but it wasn't enough.

Hawk wanted more.

And so, it seemed, did Jenny.

She touched him the way he touched her. She skimmed muscle and flesh, making his stomach quiver, his breath rush out.

This was more than sex, he thought. This was emotion, his and hers, wrapped in the texture of their lives.

Tonight they needed to expel the hurt and loneliness—the pain of her abuse, the shame of his illegitimacy.

They lay side by side, bathed in a wash of light. He brushed her cheek and leaned in close to whisper in her ear.

He spoke in the Apache tongue. He didn't know the language well, but he knew enough to speak from the heart, to tell her she would always be safe with him, that he would protect her with his life.

Their eyes met and held, and he knew she understood his words, the Chiricahua vow he'd given her.

"I trust you," she said.

He caressed her face, tracing every feature.

"Before we make love, we should purify each other," he told her, reaching for the small pot of sage on the nightstand.

She kept her eyes on his. "Just tell me what to do."

He lit the bundle and handed her a hawk feather. They knelt on the bed, and he instructed her to fan the smoke over his body.

He purified her next, and as the smoke swirled in a sweet, healing scent, he saw more than her physical beauty. Her saw her spirit, the gentleness that made her a woman.

Hawk returned the clay pot and the feather to his nightstand. He left the sage burning and reached for Jenny. Still kneeling on the bed, he kissed her.

"Tonight is magic," she said.

"Because of us. Because of this." He drew her hips to his, pressing her heat against his.

She tipped her head back, and he watched her hair spill over her shoulders and down her back. She was so beautiful.

His angel. His dove.

He tongued her ear, and when she made a soft moaning sound, he slid his hand between her legs and rubbed. She rocked against the pressure.

"Tell me what you want, Jenny. Tell me."

"You made me fly before. I want to fly again." Her voice broke with need. "I want you, Hawk." She trapped his gaze. "I want you inside me."

He reached for the dresser and battled to open the top drawer. Securing a foil packet, he tore it open and sheathed himself.

And then he lifted her hips and eased her onto his length. She took him with breathless wonder, with a penetration so deep his mind spun. The thrusts were long and slow, the kisses moist, the caresses laced with emotion. She rode him up and down in a slick, rocking motion.

And suddenly his body screamed out for more. Rearing up, he intensified the strokes and saw her eyes flash like twin jewels.

She matched his rhythm, milking him with a pulse of moonlight, a glint of stars, a sprinkle of glitter.

This was the start of their orgasm. The beginning of the flight they both craved. The unity only a man and woman could share. He slipped his fingers through hers and held tight.

Then they closed their eyes and soared into the night.

The wind raged through his lungs, as fast as a heartbeat, as cool and smooth as a rain-kissed cloud. A thrill, a sexual heat poured through his blood, filling him with greed. All he cared about was Jenny. Holding her. Being with her. Spilling into her.

She breathed his name, just his name, and he marveled at the sound, at the tender, sweet, wild way she called out to him.

Her orgasm triggered his, and he climaxed on cue, diving over the edge and into a mindless abyss.

* * *

Delightfully boneless and wonderfully sated, Jenny collapsed on top of Hawk.

After a short while he rolled to his side and sent her sliding onto the sheet.

She frowned until he snaked a protective arm around her. She wasn't ready to end the connection. She wanted to snuggle and chat about unimportant things.

She peered at his face and saw that his eyes were closed. "You're not going to sleep, are you?"

"No."

"Good."

"Why good?"

"Because I want to talk."

"About what?"

She shrugged. "I don't know."

He chuckled and opened his eyes. "I guess that's a girl thing, huh?"

She wrinkled her nose at him. "Yes. Just like rolling over and going to sleep is a guy thing."

He tweaked her wrinkled nose, coaxing a smile out of her. And at that playful moment, she decided he was the most beautiful man on earth. He'd given her everything she needed. Warmth, tenderness, passion.

"I'm not dozing off," he told her. "I still have to…" He paused and glanced down. "You know."

"Remove the condom?" she asked, amused by his sudden shyness.

"Yeah." He peeled off the latex and tossed it into a nearby trash can. "Damn things are messy," he complained when he spotted her feminine smile.

"Are they now?" She liked being this free with him, this comfortable, this intimate. "I'll be right back."

Jenny went into the bathroom and dampened a washcloth. Then she took a minute to study the masculine surroundings: the double-edged razor left carelessly on the sink, the toothpaste he'd forgotten to cap, the plain beige towels hanging haphazardly, the generic-looking shower curtain half in and half out of the tub.

Hawk was certainly a bachelor.

What would it be like to live with him? she wondered. To sleep beside him every night? To be the woman he pledged forever to?

Without thinking, she capped his toothpaste, then realized what she'd done, what she'd been fantasizing.

One step at a time, she warned herself, even though somewhere deep inside she knew she was falling in love.

Deeply, madly, crazy in love.

Dear God.

Nervous now, she paced the bathroom. Maybe this was just the afterglow of sex, the need to form an emotional attachment.

At her age? And after what she'd been through?

No, Jenny thought. Her feelings were real. Frightening, but real.

She quit pacing. She couldn't hide out for the rest of the night. She had to face Hawk.

Returning to her lover, she handed him the damp washcloth.

"What's this for?" he asked.

She sat on the edge of the bed and struggled for her next breath. "The messiness."

He laughed and pulled her onto the sheet, hugging

her playfully. The washcloth fell from his hand and landed on the floor. "Afraid I'd get you all sticky?"

"No, I…" Her heart hammered in her chest. He was still partially aroused. She could feel the power of his naked body against hers.

He straddled her, then moved in for a kiss. But when he looked into her eyes, he stopped.

"Jenny, what's wrong?"

I'm falling in love with you, she thought. And she shouldn't be. This was too soon. She was still battling the aftermath of a painful marriage and a volatile divorce. She should be exerting her independence, not falling in love.

"Jenny?"

"Nothing's wrong," she managed.

"Don't keep secrets from me, honey. Not now."

"I'm not," she lied. "I feel a little silly about the washcloth."

"I'm sorry. I didn't mean to hurt your feelings. I'm just not used to having a woman fuss over me."

"I know."

"I should have been the one bringing you a warm cloth." He shifted until she lay in the crook of his arm, warm and protected. "I should be babying you."

Jenny snuggled closer. It felt so good to be near him. "No one needs to baby anyone."

"We can stay up and talk," he said.

"That's all right. You can sleep if you're tired." Encouraging him to doze would be easier than pretending, than allowing him to question her scattered emotions.

"Are you sure you're all right?" he asked. "You don't regret what we did, do you?"

"No." She turned to look at him, to meet his worried gaze. "I wanted to be with you." And now, heaven help her, she wanted to sleep beside him every night, to wake up in his arms every morning, to make plans for an unstable future.

"I forgot about Muddy," Hawk said after a few minutes of silence. "I guess I should go get him."

He grabbed his jeans off the floor and stepped into them.

When he returned, he deposited the pup beside Jenny. Muddy made a sweet sighing sound, like a child content to be with his parents.

Hawk undressed and climbed back into bed, and after he fell asleep, Jenny lay awake in the dark, clinging to the man and the dog that had become her family.

Hawk awoke to a ringing telephone. He leaped up and grabbed it before the noise roused Jenny.

"Hello?"

"Hawk? Dusty Randall here. I have some information for you."

His brain kicked into gear. He glanced at Jenny's sleeping form and moved farther away from the bed. He knew this call was about her ex-husband. "I'm listening."

"Roy Segal is still living and working in Salt Lake City. And as far as we can tell, he isn't planning a trip to Texas."

Hawk blew out a relieved breath, and Randall continued, "But when Ms. Taylor first left Utah, he went ballistic. He threatened some of her acquaintances when they wouldn't tell him where she was."

"No one in Salt Lake City knows where she is," Hawk said, as an image of Roy going ballistic tightened his gut. "No one but the man who told her about the job at the Lone Star Country Club."

"That's right," the P.I. confirmed. "But he refused to speak to Segal."

Hawk glanced at Jenny again. The blanket draped her in a faded wash of color, and her hair spilled over the pillow like gold ribbon. Muddy, snuggled beside her, protected her with his paw.

"Then for now, everything is okay," he said.

"So it seems, but Segal has been traveling quite a bit. Just not to Texas."

"Has he been searching for her elsewhere? Did he stumble onto a false lead?"

"That's yet to be determined," Randall said. "But hopefully, we'll have more information in the next report."

Hawk cradled the phone while he slipped on a pair of jeans. "Thanks. I'll be waiting to hear from you again."

"There's one more thing."

"What's that?"

"Before Ms. Taylor left Utah, someone from Mission Creek hired an associate of ours to run a background check on her. He also had her under surveillance for a short time."

Hawk's heart slammed against his ribs. "Who? Who was checking up on Jenny?"

"Archy Wainwright," Randall said.

Son of a bitch.

"Do you want us to follow up on Mr. Wainwright's interest in her? It's probably business-related, but one can never be sure."

"I'll take care of it." Today, he thought. He'd pay Archy a visit today.

Randall ended the call, and Hawk placed the portable phone back on the charger. What if Archy's interest in Jenny wasn't business-related? What if he—

Jenny stirred, making a low, moaning sound. She opened her eyes, fluttering a set of dark lashes.

"Hi," she said, her voice laced with sleep. "You're up already?"

"Yeah. I was thinking about making a pot of coffee." And leaving a message for his father to expect him. "Do you want some?"

"Sure."

She sat up and held the blanket to her breasts. The modest gesture only added to her sensuality.

Hawk couldn't help himself. He went to her, cupped her face and kissed her as deeply as possible.

"Oh, my." Dazed and aroused, she arched like a cat. The blanket fell, revealing dusky nipples.

Hawk sucked one into his mouth, then lifted his head and kissed her again. "I wish I could stay and play today, but I have to work."

"Me, too. Will I see you tonight?"

"Yes." He reached out to hold her, to cradle her in his arms. "We'll get together later."

After he confronted Archy.

Eleven

The Wainwright spread was fifteen thousand acres. A sprawling, tree-lined driveway, flanked by a four-rail fence, led to what some folks referred to as a mansion.

The Wainwright ranch was legend in these parts, and everyone, including Hawk, knew details about it.

Longhorn cattle grazed in an abundance of green, and somewhere out back, a carefully trimmed hedge surrounded a sparkling swimming pool.

Hawk neared the house, refusing to be intimidated by its splendor, by the French doors and white decks, the picture-perfect pots of flowers, the massive lawn that hosted fancy barbecues and parties.

He parked his truck. He didn't give a rat's ass about his daddy's home. All he cared about was finding out why Archy had hired a detective agency to investigate Jenny.

A Latino woman answered the door.

"My name is Hawk. Archy Wainwright is expecting me," he told her, assuming a rigid, don't-even-think-of-turning-me-away stance.

She nodded and invited him inside. He didn't hesitate, but he didn't enjoy crossing the threshold he used to wonder about as a child. There was a time when he *had* given a damn about this mansion, when it had mattered more than anything.

An impressive foyer led to a staircase paving the way to the bedrooms his half siblings had most likely slept in each night.

He knew their names—Justin, Rose and Susan. One brother and two sisters. He glanced at the staircase again and realized that Susan, his younger sister, hadn't spent her childhood here. Archy's ex-wife had whisked her away to Houston when Hawk's existence had become known.

"This way."

The housekeeper ushered him into a room decorated in rich woods and maroon carpeting. Although the decor was luxurious, it wasn't stiff or cold. And to top it off, a floor-to-ceiling window presented a picture-postcard display of the South Texas landscape.

Hawk had wanted the house to seem brittle, and the idyllic view bothered him more than he cared to admit.

The woman gestured to a sofa, but he shook his head. He preferred to stand.

When he squared his shoulders, she caught his gaze. Quite obviously, she knew who he was. Like everyone else in Mission Creek, she'd probably heard the nasty rumors about him.

"Mr. Wainwright will be with you shortly."

"Thanks."

The housekeeper left the room. Hawk didn't pace, and he didn't touch anything. He just waited, his emotions deep and dark and riddled with pain.

Archy arrived several minutes later, making a lord-of-the-ranch entrance: a custom hat, a well-tailored Western shirt, a trophy buckle as big as the Lone Star State itself.

He took in Hawk's appearance through steely blue eyes, and they stared each other down.

Today Hawk wore his turquoise nugget around his neck and a favored pair of moccasins on his feet. He'd chosen both with Archy in mind, deliberately reminding his father that his bastard son was an Apache.

"So what's this all about?" Archy asked. "Did you change your mind about the work I offered you?"

"No," Hawk replied, doing his damnedest to keep his emotions in check. He hated his father with a passion he could barely contain, and standing here in his house made the hatred even stronger.

The older man cocked his head. "Then can I assume you're in some sort of trouble?"

"Trouble?"

Archy waved his hand, a gesture of authority, of impatience. "Don't mess with me, boy. Just tell me want you're after. Because if it's money—"

"I told you before. I don't want your money. Not in the form of a paycheck or in the form of a handout. This isn't about money. This is about Jenny."

"Jenny?" Archy stepped forward. "Is she all right?"

"I'm looking after her," Hawk said.

"Meaning what? That you're sleeping with her? That you finally got her into bed?"

Hawk clenched his fist, wishing he could ram it straight down his father's throat. "And why should that matter to you? Were you hoping to lure her into *your* bed? The way you did my mother?"

Archy spewed out a vile curse. "First of all, I won't discuss Rain Dancer with you. And secondly, where in the hell did you get a notion that I had designs on Jenny? For Pete's sake, she's young enough to be my daughter.''

"You hired a P.I. to run a background check on her. You had her under surveillance."

"I had her investigated for the club. An associate of mine referred her, but he also said that she appeared to be having some personal difficulties. So I decided to learn more about her before I recommended her to the architect in charge of the renovations.''

Hawk's gaze was unflinching, but so was Archy's. "What did you learn about her?" he asked.

"The same things you must already know. She's an only child, and both her parents are dead. She was married and divorced, but her husband had a tough time letting her go. She was a victim of domestic violence, but she never reported the abuse. During the divorce, she petitioned for a restraining order, then dropped the charges, most likely because she was afraid to face Roy Segal in court.''

Hawk had to stop his equilibrium from spinning. Archy had known about Jenny's hardship all along.

"I debated on whether or not to offer her the job," the older man said. "I was concerned about her exhusband showing up at the club and creating some sort of spectacle. But in the end I decided that she probably needed a fresh start. So I caved in and called her.''

"And when she arrived at Mission Creek, you took a deeper interest in her.''

Archy frowned. "Yes. But not in a sexual way. I wanted to protect her, I suppose. Although she was quite professional, I knew she was lost. She seemed like she needed someone. A father figure, if you will.''

A father figure? Hawk took a step back. How could Archy put himself in that light?

Because Archy cared about Jenny, he thought. And he'd gone out of his way to help her, proving he had a heart.

Confused, Hawk stood in the luxurious room, staring at his dad, and then a woman entered the scene and broke the silence.

''Archy, have you seen Justin? He was supposed to meet me…''

Her words died when she spotted Hawk. She glanced at Archy, then back at Hawk.

''Oh, God,'' she said.

''Kate.'' Archy tried to approach her, but she held him off.

''Don't,'' she told him, raising a trembling hand. ''Don't.''

Hawk didn't know what to do, especially when she moved toward him. He knew who she was now.

Kate Wainwright. Archy's ex-wife.

He had never met her before, but now he could see every feature: light-green eyes, narrow nose, medium-brown hair perfectly coiffed. She stood slim and lithe, the picture of elegance and style.

Was she his mother's rival? This lady staring at him as if he was a ghost?

''You look like her,'' Kate said. ''You look like Rain Dancer. But you look like Archy, too.'' She turned to her ex-husband then. ''He's your son, damn you. He's your son.''

''No, he isn't.''

''Yes, he is,'' she insisted, tears clouding her eyes.

Hawk felt his stomach tighten, his heart go numb. Once again Archy had denounced him. He hurt so badly he could barely breathe.

And Kate, the woman Archy had cheated on, was hurting, too.

"I'm sorry," Hawk said, his apology barely audible.

"This isn't your fault," she whispered back. Her tears fell in earnest now, and he knew why.

Kate Wainwright still loved her ex-husband.

Hawk felt as if the walls were closing in. The bookcase shifting, the French window collapsing, the panes of glass shattering with each breath he took. He had to get the hell out of here.

He moved away from Kate and stopped directly in front of Archy.

"When I was little, I wanted you to be my father," he said, his voice tight. "I even included you in my prayers. But that was a long time ago. I despise you now, and I'll despise you until my dying day."

Archy flinched, but he didn't respond.

Hawk bumped the older man's shoulder and left the Wainwright mansion without looking back.

Jenny could see the torment in her lover's eyes, sense the pain and anger brewing in his heart.

And she felt responsible.

He'd gone to Archy's house because of her. He'd put himself in an uncomfortable situation on her behalf. And that situation had escalated into emotional warfare—a battle Hawk would never win.

He prowled her living room like a restless predator, a warrior stalking an invisible enemy.

"I'm sorry," she said.

He stopped to drag a hand through his hair, which flowed down his back, as dark and fluid as the night.

"This isn't your fault," he told her, and then a frown marred his brow. "You know what? Kate said the same exact thing to me. 'This isn't your fault.'"

"You weren't the one who made her cry, Hawk."

"Yes, I am. I'm the living, breathing proof of her husband's affair." He reached for one of the dining-room chairs and turned it around. Straddling it, he shook his head. "Can you believe she still loves him?"

Jenny didn't know what to say. Hawk wasn't just suffering from his father's rejection. He struggled with a newly acquired guilt. He'd met Kate Wainwright, the woman his mother had wronged. In spite of how young and naive Rain Dancer had been, she'd willingly slept with Kate's husband, something Hawk couldn't seem to make excuses for anymore. Kate was real to him now. He'd seen her pain firsthand.

"I'm so confused," he said.

"I know." Jenny studied his posture, the strong arms banded around the back of the chair, the long, muscled legs bent at the knees.

God, she loved him. She loved him more than she'd ever dreamed of loving Roy. This man was her hope, her heart, her salvation.

Yet she feared the feeling, the need clawing inside her, a need as sharp and edgy as the talons he wore.

"Tell me what's going on in your mind," Hawk said. "This affects you, too."

"What do you mean?"

"Is this going to make being around Archy more difficult for you?"

"Of course it is. He hurt the man…" The man I love, she thought. "He hurt you, Hawk."

"Yes, but do you realize how much my father cares about you, Jenny?"

She nodded. "Still, to be honest, I'm having a little trouble coming to terms with him knowing my past." Keeping secrets was easier for her. She'd lived most of her adult life in secret.

"Really? As difficult as this has been, that part makes me feel better. The P.I. said you should tell people about Roy. Archy already knows, so that seems like a step in the right direction."

"But look at all the pain it's caused. You confronted Archy about me, and you ended up getting hurt in the process."

"I'll get over it."

No, he wouldn't. What happened today had left another gouge, another permanent scar on his life. And she wanted to help. She wanted to comfort him. Yet deep down she knew Archy was the only person who could heal Hawk's wounds. "It isn't fair."

When he didn't respond, she left her spot on the couch.

Standing in front of him, she said, "Please, Hawk, tell me what I can do to make you feel better."

He rose to his feet and moved the chair he'd been straddling. "You can touch me, Jenny." He took her hands and pressed them against his heart.

This was a balm, she thought. A temporary fix. But it was all she had to give, and she gave willingly.

She kissed him until she tasted his pain, until he held her tight against his body and let the hurt turn to hunger.

The instant they separated, they started peeling off

their clothes. His jeans and shirt landed on top of the coffee table, and her dress made its way to the discarded dining-room chair. He secured a condom from his wallet and smiled at her.

"I came prepared."

"You're all I think about," she said, rubbing her nakedness against his. "You're all I want."

"Me, too."

The blinds were open, but the lace curtains were drawn. Jenny could see small bits of light shining through them. To her, they looked like stars—sparks of silver and shimmers of gold.

Hawk told her to make a wish, and she gazed at him in wonder.

"How do you do that?" she asked, skimming a fingernail down his chest.

"Do what?"

"Read my mind."

"I read the look in your eyes, the magic that's always been there. You bewitch me, Jenny."

She kissed him, and they sank to the carpet to make love on the floor.

Glorious, wild, soul-searching love.

They rolled in each other's arms, caressing, touching, quivering, panting. He slid his hand between her legs; she kissed his neck and felt his blood pulse through his veins.

He tasted like desire, like a man who needed more. So much more.

She moved down his body, and he made a sound of arousal, a groan of masculine surrender.

Her hair spilled over his thighs. She paused to look up at him and saw that he watched.

"I'm so turned on," he said.

"I know." And she reveled in his pleasure, in the need flashing in his eyes. He was magic, too. This man who'd offered to protect her with his life.

Jenny teased him with her tongue, kissing and licking.

He smoothed her hair away from her face, and she realized the gold-streaked strands had obstructed his view.

Apparently he didn't want to miss a moment of his seduction.

Giving him what he craved, she took him into her mouth. He lifted his hips and focused on every move she made.

She loved him thoroughly, with her mouth, with her heart, with a rhythm that had him chanting her name.

"You have to stop," he growled suddenly. "Jenny, you have to stop."

She pressed her cheek against his thigh and smiled up at him. "I don't have to do anything."

"Yes, you do."

"No, I don't."

She put her mouth on him again, but he pulled her up, rolled her over and straddled her in one swift, decided move.

"This isn't the time to show me how rebellious you are. I'm barely holding on." He cursed and scouted the floor for the condom.

Jenny found it first.

"Don't play around," he warned.

Brimming with newfound power, she fought the temptation to lower her head, to finish what she'd started.

He grabbed the foil out of her hand, his voice fighting for control. "I need you so badly, honey. But if you tell me to stop, I will. Or if I get too rough…"

"Don't hold back. Don't ever hold back." Jenny wanted to feel his passion. "I trust you, Hawk."

In the next instant he was sheathed inside her, thrusting hard and deep, making them both crazy with desire.

A climactic moan escaped her throat. A pulse pounded between her legs, and she arched against the pressure, taking him even deeper.

This was need. This was love. This was sex so intense, she couldn't tell where her body ended and his began.

"What would I do without you?" he asked. "How would I survive?"

She couldn't respond. She'd lost the ability to think, to talk, to do anything but feel his body pumping into hers.

His skin was hot and damp. She ran her hands all over him, over hard angles and smooth planes, over muscle and sinew.

And then she wrapped her legs around him.

Tightly. As tightly as she could manage.

Braced above her, he lowered his head, and they kissed, over and over, tongues colliding.

Jenny never wanted this feeling, this wild glory, to end.

"Me, neither," he said.

She skimmed his cheek, his cleanly shaven jaw. "You read my mind again."

"I see it in your eyes."

"Can we do this every day?" she asked as he rocked her body. "Can we make love every day?"

"Every hour," he said, pushing deeper. "Every minute."

He threw back his head, and she knew he was going to climax.

Her mate. Her warrior.

He spilled his seed, and she clung to him desperately, wishing the wetness could flow through her. The wetness that would give her a baby.

Hawk's baby.

She looked up at him. He stared back at her.

"Your turn," he said, slipping his hand between their bodies.

She couldn't stop it from happening. Nor did she want to. She edged closer and closer to the orgasm he was determined to give her.

Her mind spun, her pulse raced out of control. She closed her eyes and let herself fall.

Deeper in love.

And deeper into the fantasy of having his child.

Twelve

Morning brought a ray of sunshine, but Hawk couldn't concentrate on anything other than his emotions. Panic rose like a torrid, turbulent tide.

He couldn't lie to himself or to Jenny. He had to give credence to his feelings. He had to tag them, to name them, to tell Jenny what was happening.

But he feared the worst. He feared rejection.

Alone in her kitchen, he poured himself a cup of coffee. He'd made it strong. Too strong, he supposed.

"Hawk?"

He started at the sound of Jenny's voice, sending the hot drink sloshing over his hand. Turning, he blew on his fingers like a kid who didn't have enough sense to subdue the burn with something cold.

"What happened?" she asked.

"Nothing. I just spilled my coffee."

She was so damn beautiful, he thought. Her hair fell in golden disarray, and a silky nightgown, rivaling the color of her eyes, streamed over fluid curves.

His woman. His lover.

"You should rinse your hand," she said.

"I'm fine." And to prove his point, he lifted his cup and ignored the blister already forming.

Arching like a tabby, she stretched lazily.

His gaze roamed over her, alighting on the outline of her nipples, on the shadow between her legs. She hadn't worn panties to bed last night, and now he wanted to lift her onto the counter, unzip his jeans and slide into her warm, wet heat.

Air hissed from his lungs, but he tempered the rush of excitement, the arousal nipping at his common sense. This wasn't the time for sex.

Before he spilled his coffee again, he took a guarded step back.

"Will you pour me a cup?" she asked, oblivious to his distress.

"Sure." He cursed his unsteady hands. "It's a little strong, but I can dilute it for you."

"Thanks." She brushed by him to put bread in the toaster.

They'd fallen into a morning routine already, he noted. As he doctored her coffee with cream and sugar, she buttered his toast with jam.

They'd been friends before lovers. And that, he suspected, made the difference.

She sliced a banana, spun around to sip her sweetened coffee and finished throwing together a quick and easy breakfast. But as she prepared to set the table, he stopped her.

He didn't want to stay in the house. He needed air, lots of fresh air. "Let's eat outside."

"Okay. Just let me get my robe."

She disappeared and returned with a matching robe. He watched her arrange their meal on a tray, thinking how festive she made instant oatmeal look. He grabbed the finished product and escorted her onto the patio, where Muddy waited at the door.

The dog greeted them as if he'd been stranded for hours, when in fact, Hawk had shoved the pooch outside not more than twenty minutes before.

He set the tray on a glass-topped table and studied the squirming mutt. "Don't look at me like that. You haven't been out here that long. Nobody abandoned you."

Muddy barked in response. Woof. *You could have fooled me.*

Hawk frowned. "I'll bet you didn't even go."

Woof. *I did, too.* Muddy ran to the edge of the fence where a fresh puddle lay, proving he'd done what he was supposed to do.

"Okay, my mistake." Hawk glanced at Jenny and found her watching him with an amused expression. "You think this is funny?" he asked as the dog nearly stepped in his own pee.

"It's cute," she said. "You and Muddy are cute together."

"Oh." Embarrassed, he shrugged, then caught the edge of her smile. Instantly his heartbeat staggered, and his knees went wobbly.

How could one fragile woman turn a big, broad-shouldered guy to mush? he asked himself, knowing damn well he was lost.

Muddy settled down with a rawhide treat, and Jenny and Hawk sat across from each other. Potted plants hung from the slatted roof, decorating the patio with leaves and flowers.

"What do you want to do today?" she asked.

Go back to bed, he thought. Fill the ache, the need to hold her and never let go.

"Talk," he said.

"About what?" She spooned a glob of oatmeal into her mouth and waited for him to answer.

"Us."

Her eyes grew wide. "What about us?"

He pushed the pent-up breath from his lungs, wishing he knew how to say what was on his mind. He'd never been good at expressing his feelings. He felt as if he was about to cut open a vein and bleed all over her nice white table.

"Damn it," he said.

"Why are you cursing? What's wrong?"

"Nothing. Oh, hell. I'm in love with you, Jenny," he blurted. "And I'm scared out of my wits."

If her eyes hadn't been attached to her sockets, they would have popped out of her head. She just stared at him, like an elf owl stunned into silence.

Smooth, he thought, cursing his stupidity. Real smooth.

"Why are you scared?" she finally managed.

Lifting one shoulder in a partial shrug, he tried to act more casual than he felt. Her owlish reaction wasn't easing his panic. In his culture owls represented ghosts. He'd had to learn to accept their presence without spooking every time they screeched.

"Because I'm worried about how you feel about me. You've been through a rough ordeal, and you're probably not ready to get overly attached."

"Yes, I am."

"You are?"

"Yes."

"Really? You're not just saying that?"

"No." She held his gaze from across the table, her voice quavering. "I love you, too, Hawk."

Dear God. He hadn't expected this. Hadn't even dreamed it was possible. And now he didn't know what to do or what to say. So he just sat there, dumbfounded.

"I feel like I've got frogs in my stomach," he admitted finally.

"Me, too. But mine are more like butterflies."

He supposed butterflies were more feminine than frogs, but the idea of insects and amphibians popping around in their bellies didn't make being in love seem very romantic.

"What are we supposed to do now?" he asked.

She twisted her napkin on her lap. "I don't know."

"We could hug." It was the only suggestion that came to his shell-shocked mind, the only physical contact that seemed remotely possible.

A breeze lifted her napkin. The paper corners flapped, rustling beneath her fingers. "Should I come over there?"

"If you want to." It wasn't supposed to be like this, was it? He wasn't an authority on matters of the heart, but this didn't seem normal.

She left her chair, then stood beside him, gnawing her bottom lip nervously.

"You're scared, too," he said.

She nodded. "I wasn't going to tell you how I felt. I was going to keep it a secret."

"Why?"

"Because that's what I do. I keep secrets."

She swayed, and he reached for her, easing her onto his lap. She put her head on his shoulder, and he rocked her. When she closed her eyes and cooed, he knew the dove in her had broken free.

This was a turning point for her, he thought. She trusted him enough to love him, to give him part of her soul—the part another man had all but destroyed.

She lifted her head to look at him, her eyes shimmering with tears. "I can't believe this is happening."

"I know." Hawk drew a deep breath, struggling to grasp the enormity, the intensity of their emotions. "I wasn't prepared to fall in love, to feel this kind of desperation. I'm not even sure when it happened. One day I was watching my pretty neighbor plant flowers, and a few weeks later I'm aching inside."

She rubbed her cheek against his, and the whiskers scraped her skin. He wanted to apologize for the roughness, but he smoothed a hand down her hair, instead.

"It happened to me after we made love the first time," she said. "I went into the bathroom to dampen a washcloth and fell apart."

"Next time I'll use the washcloth." He inhaled her scent, the raspberry mist melding with the morning air. "Next time I'll let you rub it all over my body."

A dreamy sound escaped her lips, and he lifted her into his arms and carried her into the house. Muddy followed, tracking them with a rawhide chew sticking out of the corner of his mouth.

"Let's go back to bed for a while," Hawk said. To hold each other, he thought. To get used to butterflies and frogs and the feeling of being in love.

The following afternoon Jenny came to an important decision. And now all she had to do was tell Hawk.

She sat on the edge of the bed and twisted her hands in her lap. He'd gone back to his own house to change. He'd been sleeping at her place for the past two days, shifting back and forth to shower and shave, but he was due to return any minute.

So don't dawdle, she told herself, popping up to band her hair into a ponytail. Standing in front of a beveled mirror, she checked her appearance.

The doorbell pealed, and she scrambled to the living room in one mad dash. Aside from Hawk, who'd taken her keys to let himself back in, she wasn't expecting company.

She answered the summons and found her lover standing on the porch. Tall and sexy, with his Stetson dipped low on his forehead and a smile softening the scar near his mouth, he leaned forward for a kiss.

His lips touched hers, and she clung to him nervously.

"Hi," he said, nipping her jaw.

"Hi." Tempering her emotions, she found a steady voice. "Why did you ring the bell?"

"Because I forgot to take your keys with me when I went home this morning."

"Then it's time I made you a spare." They both knew why her door must remained locked. Roy was still a threat, and he probably always would be. She'd gotten a post-office box and a cell phone, but there was more she needed to do to protect herself.

"Are you ready?" he asked.

"Almost."

He stepped into the house and ran his gaze over her. "You look ready."

"I am. I mean, I'm all dressed and everything, but there's something I need to get off my chest before we go."

The Stetson didn't hide his frown or the sudden concern in his eyes. "What's going on?"

She leaned against the back of a cushioned chair.

"I'm going to tell the neighbors about Roy. And once I tackle that, I'll join a support group."

He reached out to stroke her cheek, to run his callused fingers over her skin. "What made you change your mind?"

"Us," she answered honestly. "We can't have a healthy future if I'm still battling the past."

"That means more to me than you can possibly know. I've been so worried about you, Jenny."

"I know." She absorbed his caress, thinking how much she loved him. "But I have to admit, the idea of talking to strangers about my life still makes me nervous."

"You'll get through it, and I'll be by your side. I promise."

"I'll talk to Mrs. Pritchett first, but I don't want to do it today. I just want to go horseback riding and have a good time."

"No problem." He took her hand, and they left the house—and her anxiety—behind.

An hour later Hawk gave Jenny a tour of Jackson Stables. The barn he leased was equipped with ten stalls, a large feed room, a tidy office and a tack room stocked with saddles, bits, bridles and grooming supplies.

"I'm impressed," she said.

"Thanks." He reached for a saddle and transferred it into her arms. "I think this one ought to fit you."

Jenny balanced the offering, eager to ride. Hawk gathered his tack and they headed outdoors.

The sun greeted them with a pale-yellow glow, and shadows from the trees dappled the ground, sending leafy patterns across the soil.

Jenny's mount, a buckskin gelding named Sonny's

Gold, stood patiently at the hitching post. Hawk had arranged for her to ride his best trail horse, and Jenny couldn't help but appreciate Sonny's eager-to-please personality and easy disposition.

"Ready?" Hawk asked when both horses were tacked up.

"Yes." Jenny was more than ready. She climbed into the saddle and adjusted the stirrups. She'd taken riding lessons during college, and she missed the serenity of a long, dusty trail.

Hawk mounted a flashy black gelding, and she took a moment to admire man and beast.

The man boasted a warrior's face and a strong, muscular body. The beast, blessed with his own form of beauty, tossed his head arrogantly, as if he knew he was as regal as his master.

"What's his name?" Jenny asked.

"I call him Night."

She scanned the animal's sleek black coat and flowing ebony mane. "It suits him. You've had him a long time, haven't you?"

"Yes. We've been partners for years."

A spiritual attachment, she thought, that made the Apache and his horse seem like one being.

Hawk reined Night toward the hills, and Jenny and Sonny followed.

They headed down a wide, colorful path. The recent rain enriched the elements, making the ground shimmer. Grass grew in green and gold patches, and stones scattered the earth in flecks of gray.

A mild breeze blew, stirring Hawk's hair beneath his hat. It looked like a raven's wing, smooth and dark and poised for flight.

They traveled for hours, making small talk, and when they reached a stream, Hawk suggested a break.

"This is my favorite spot," he said.

"I can see why. Is it still private property?"

He nodded. "Jackson Stables owns quite a bit of land."

Gripping her waist, he helped her dismount. She leaned into him and let his body warm hers.

"You have a good seat, Jenny. You ride well."

"Thank you." She turned to meet his gaze, and they held each other. Today was the start of a new life, she thought. The dawn of change.

Hawk released her to tend to the horses. Afterward, he walked to the edge of the stream. Squatting, he skimmed his hand across the surface, making a swishing sound. Silent, Jenny knelt beside him.

A movement in the sky caught her attention, and she glanced up.

A large bird danced on the air currents. She watched it, noting the angle of its wings.

"It's a red-tailed hawk," he said, drying his hand on his jeans. "But it's still young."

"How can you tell?"

"That it's a red-tail or that it's young?"

She kept her eye on the raptor, watching its sweeping flight. "Both."

"The marks on the underwing identify the species. And I can tell it hasn't obtained its adult plumage by its tail. See the dark bands? That's a sign of an immature red-tail. An adult would have its color."

"When do they get their adult plumage?" she asked, shifting her gaze to the human hawk.

"In their first molt, when they're a year old. But they don't reach sexual maturity until they're three."

His eyes locked onto hers. "Once they mate, they bond for life. Just like doves," he added softy.

He plucked a small white flower and handed it to her. Touched by the gesture, she clutched it to her heart, wishing this moment could last forever.

On Monday morning Hawk and Jenny sat on her porch discussing Randall's latest report.

"It seems Roy is searching for you," Hawk said, repeating what the P.I. had told him. "Apparently Roy thinks you're in Arizona or New Mexico, because he's been concentrating heavily on those regions, checking out design firms there."

She let out a ragged breath. "He knows how influenced I am by Southwestern architecture. Of course, he's aware that I have a fascination with the Old West, too."

"According to Randall, Roy seems convinced that you're working for someone else. I guess he didn't figure that you'd start your own business."

"I wish he'd fall off the face of the earth," she said.

"Me, too." But her ex-husband wasn't going to disappear, and they both knew it. Hawk studied her. He and Jenny were both dressed for work, but the idea of spending eight hours away from her every day made him uneasy. How long would it take for Roy to discover her whereabouts? A week? A month? A year? "I think I should give the sheriff a call. It wouldn't hurt to let him know what's going on."

Her eyes grew wide. "You mean Justin Wainwright?"

"He is the sheriff."

"He's also your half brother. Won't that make you uncomfortable?"

Yes, he thought, the idea of calling Justin, one of Archy's legitimate sons, made him uncomfortable as hell. "I'm not inviting him out for a beer. This is your safety we're talking about."

"There's nothing the sheriff can do, is there?"

"Not at this point. Randall is documenting his findings, but for the time being, Roy hasn't broken any laws." Hawk shifted his weight and stretched his legs out in front of him. "But we both know that if Roy shows up in Mission Creek, he'll cause trouble. I want the sheriff to be ready."

"I'll go to court this time," she said. "I won't back down."

Good girl, he thought, admiring the determined tilt of her chin.

Jenny turned to gaze across the street. "I should probably talk to Mrs. Pritchett today. I suppose I could do it now."

"Should I stay here?" he asked. "Or do you want me to go with you?"

She reached for his hand. "I want you with me. Oh, Hawk, I really hate this. I hate everyone knowing everything about me."

Because he didn't know how else to comfort her, he raised their joined hands and brushed his lips across her knuckles. In response she managed a small, shaky smile.

A few minutes later they knocked on their neighbor's door.

Mrs. Pritchett answered, wearing one of her frumpy housecoats. She peered at Jenny and then at Hawk, a pair of silver-framed reading glasses perched on her nose.

"What are you doing here?" she asked, keeping her gaze trained on Hawk. Her eyes narrowed into beady slits.

Since Hawk tended to associate people with birds, he decided she fit the image of a snippy old crow. "Jenny and I would like to talk to you."

"About what?"

"My ex-husband," Jenny said, squeezing Hawk's hand.

"Is that so?" As expected, curiosity gleamed. "I wasn't aware you had been married."

"My husband was abusive and controlling, so I divorced him. He started stalking me. I managed to get away, but we have reason to believe that he's searching for me." She drew a breath and let it out slowly. "We wanted you to be aware of who he is in case he shows up."

"Oh, my." Mrs. Pritchett placed a hand over her heart. "Why don't you come in, dear, and fill me in on the details?" She snorted at Hawk then. "You can come in, too, I suppose. But I'm not fixing you any tea."

For Jenny's sake, Hawk held his tongue. He gave the older woman a tight nod and entered her house.

Jenny clung to his hand, and they were ushered into a living room as dated as Mrs. Pritchett's housecoat. She directed Jenny to an avocado-colored sofa, then bustled into the kitchen. Hawk assumed he wasn't welcome to sit, so he leaned against the fireplace mantel.

"I'm sorry," Jenny whispered.

He shrugged and smiled. "I prefer coffee, any-way."

Mrs. Pritchett returned with a floral-printed teapot and two delicate cups. She poured the steaming brew and offered Jenny milk and sugar.

"Now, tell me his name and what he looks like, dear."

Jenny lifted her cup, and Hawk saw that her hand shook. He knew how difficult this was for her, and he prayed his presence gave her some measure of se-curity.

"His name is Roy Segal," she told the woman. "He's forty years old, with a medium build and light-brown hair graying at the temples. He prefers suits and sport coats. I used to think he was distinguished and handsome, but I've lost my objectivity."

"Do you have a picture of him?"

"No, but there's one on his Web site. He's owns a travel agency."

"I don't have a computer. Will you get me a copy of it?"

"Yes."

Jenny glanced back at Hawk, and he stepped for-ward to hunker down beside her. Mrs. Pritchett shifted her gaze between them.

"We appreciate your help," he said.

She gave him a pointed look. "I don't like men who abuse women."

"Neither do I," he returned. "And if Roy Segal tries to hurt Jenny again, I'll kill him."

"Well then, I suppose she's lucky you came along," Mrs. Pritchett said, stunning him speechless.

"Apparently she needs a guardian angel, even one as rough and ill-mannered as you."

Hawk merely nodded, accepting the old woman's compliment, if indeed it could be called that, with an odd sense of pride.

Thirteen

Archy hated hospitals. He hated the squeak of the nurse's rubber shoes, the pervasive smell of antiseptic, the knowledge that people lay sick and dying.

Anchored to a sterile waiting room, he sat motionless in a stiff chair. But he wasn't alone. His family surrounded him, and so did his enemies, the Carsons.

Archy glanced at Kate, his ex-wife. She sat next to him, twisting her hands in her lap. Their daughter Rose had fallen ill, with symptoms that could have easily been mistaken for the flu. But once her fever had spiked, she'd been rushed to the hospital.

Archy reached for Kate's hand and held it tightly in his. Rose was in danger. She'd contracted a life-threatening bacterial infection. Rose's infant son, Wayne Matthew Carson, had been hospitalized, as well. As of yet, he was symptom free, but that didn't mean he wasn't at risk. Everyone who'd come into close contact with Rose had been treated with a preventative antibiotic, but the doctor wanted to run some tests on the baby and monitor him. He was, after all, only an infant, with a tiny immune system.

Rose's husband, thirty-three-year-old Matt Carson, paced the waiting room. The boy looked haggard, Archy thought. Shadows dogged his eyes, and the lines around his mouth tensed with each frantic step he took. Archy had never much cared for him, though he hadn't exactly given the young man a chance. His being a Carson was enough to make him an enemy.

But now Archy viewed him in a different light. He saw how much Matt loved Rose. If Matt lost his wife and baby, he'd lose his heart. Archy wanted to go to him, put his hand reassuringly on the boy's shoulder, but he didn't want to let go of Kate. He knew his ex-wife needed him. And God help him, he needed her, too.

How much more could they take? Last fall they'd seen their other daughter, Susan, through a heart transplant. And now this.

Archy took an aching breath. He stole a tender glance at Susan and the man she'd married. She'd come through her ordeal with a new heart and a new husband. Would Rose fare as well? Would her baby boy remain healthy and strong?

Archy turned to look at his son Justin. All his children were here. No, not all of his children, he realized. There was one missing.

Dear God. Was this his punishment? His sentence for denying his own flesh and blood?

I'll make it up to Hawk, he thought, suddenly willing to tempt fate. I'll atone for my sins. Just spare Rose and the baby, and I'll do the right thing.

Checking the clock on the wall, Archy counted down the hours, his soul steeped in fear. They'd been here for what seemed an eternity. An entire day of waiting and wondering, of shifting between home and the hospital. Soon the test results should be in on the baby, as it took nearly twenty-four hours for the bacteria to grow in a lab.

Please, he prayed. Don't let my grandson take ill. And don't let my daughter die. My beautiful Rose.

Rose's husband continued to pace. Ford and Grace Carson watched their son, their faces grim. Unlike Archy and Kate, Ford and Grace remained happily married. He envied them that, but the other man hadn't betrayed his wife the way Archy had.

Ford looked up, catching Archy's gaze. They hadn't spoken to each other once during this long, agonizing wait. They were in-laws, but years of hatred separated them.

"We should pray," Grace said. "All of us together."

"Yes," Kate agreed, her voice raw with emotion. "This feud isn't doing anyone any good. We have to draw strength from each other. For Rose," she added. "And the baby."

Silence engulfed the room. Matt stopped pacing. He and the other Carson siblings looked at their father. Susan and Justin studied Archy.

Ford and Archy. Respective clan patriarchs. The choice was theirs.

Doing what must be done, Archy rose from his chair. Ford stood, too. Both stepped forward to shake hands—and to put an end to an age-old feud.

"We could get a drink at the club sometime," Ford said.

"Sure." Archy cleared his throat. "To toast our grandchild." Should the infant remain well, he thought, his chest tightening.

Ford's oldest son, Flynt, made the next move. He offered Justin the empty seat beside him. Justin nodded and sat next to his former rival.

Matt said a quiet thank-you to both families, and the Wainwrights and Carsons began to pray.

Hours later, when the doctor entered the waiting

room, Matt jumped up, followed by Archy and Kate. The young physician gave them a collective nod.

"Your wife is stable," he said to Matt. "She's going to pull through this just fine. And your son's tests came back negative. There isn't any sign of infection."

Archy let out the breath he'd been holding and silently thanked God for answering their prayers.

Later than evening Archy drove Kate back to the guest house on the ranch. They sat quietly in his car for a moment, grateful their daughter and her infant son were safe.

Kate glanced out the window, and Archy leaned back against the seat. They hadn't gotten the opportunity to see Rose, but it felt good to know she was on her way to recovery. The baby had been released to his father, with instructions to watch him carefully and bring him to the doctor next week for a follow-up examination. It was doubtful, they'd been told, that the child would fall ill during the incubation period, but Archy appreciated the precautions being taken.

"Do you want to come in?" Kate asked. "I can fix some sandwiches."

"That's sounds nice." Archy hadn't eaten all day, and he wanted to be near Kate.

They entered her house, and she went straight to the kitchen. He sat in the breakfast nook and watched her. Kate traveled between Houston and Mission Creek, but lately she'd been spending more and more time in Mission Creek. He could still remember the day she'd left him, the day she'd taken their youngest daughter and walked away.

"I'm sorry," he said.

She looked up. "For what?"

"For giving you cause to divorce me."

The butter knife in her hand nearly slipped. She stood at the butcher-block island, spreading mayonnaise on whole-wheat bread. "You mean for sleeping with another woman?"

He nodded. He'd never openly admitted his affair with Rain Dancer, but Kate had known just the same. She had never believed his denials, his self-disgusted lies.

"Why did you do it?" she asked, her voice quiet. "Why did you betray me?"

"Because I thought you were cheating on me. You were so busy, working on one charity event after another, and I suspected it was a ruse to cover up your affair. And then I saw you with Thomas Jacobson at a luncheon, and you two seemed so…close. I was sure he was the one."

"Thomas Jacobson? That young attorney from Austin?" She shook her head. "He used to ask me for advice. He was in love with Gail Millstone, and he thought I could help him win her over. Gail and I were friends at the time."

Archy pushed out of his chair and crossed to his ex-wife. "But I didn't know that, not until after I'd slept with Rain Dancer."

Kate's features tightened. "You could have talked to me. You could have asked me point-blank if I was having an affair."

"Yes, I could have, but that wasn't my way."

"Your way was to sleep with another woman."

"Yes. Something I've regretted ever since. I never stopped loving you, Kate. And I couldn't bear what I'd done. So I kept it a secret."

She opened a package of roast-beef slices, her

hands trembling. "And that secret produced a child." She looked up and snared his gaze. "Admit it, Archy. He's your son."

"Yes," he said, recalling the vow he'd made at the hospital. "Hawk is my son."

Her eyes misted. "Why didn't you tell me the truth before now?"

He struggled to explain his logic, the lie that governed his life. "I thought denying it would make it disappear."

Stunned, she stared at him. "You thought Hawk would disappear? He's a person, with a heart and a soul. Blood flows through his veins. *Your* blood."

"I know, but he was proof of my affair. The reason I lost you."

"You lost me because you cheated. And on top of that, you lied about it. You never considered my feelings or how much the truth might have meant." Her eyes drilled into his gaze, her voice edged with pain. "You never apologized. You never came to me pleading for forgiveness. I had no idea you were sorry. You seemed like a ruthless bastard."

"Maybe I was a ruthless bastard. Maybe I deserved what I got."

"You did," she said quietly. "You did."

He swallowed the lump of shame in his throat. "There's something else I need to tell you. Something I did while I was still married to you. And it concerns Hawk."

She shook her head. "Another secret, Archy?"

"Yes." Another guilty secret he had been keeping all these years.

Jenny reclined on her sofa, a stack of library books beside her on the coffee table. Hawk had asked her to accompany him next week to an educational presentation he was giving at an elementary school, and she intended to be well prepared.

Book in hand, she glanced at the VCR clock. Hawk was running late. She missed him when they weren't together, but they were still living day by day, bouncing back and forth between each other's houses. Jenny wanted to marry him, to share the same residence, to make plans for the future, but she wasn't brave enough to tell him. Besides, shouldn't a man bring up marriage first?

The front door opened, and Jenny righted her posture. Hawk didn't ring the bell anymore. He always used his key.

As his footsteps echoed on the tiled foyer, she took an eager breath. She'd come to know the familiar sound of his walk, the long, Texas stride.

He turned into the living room. "Hey, pretty lady."

"Hi." Her pulse fluttered, and the marriage fantasy pulsed through her in a warm, steady rhythm. He still wore his work clothes, a rough ensemble of denim and leather. All male and all muscle, she thought, wrapped in one tall, trail-dusty package.

He sat next to her and gestured at her reading material. "What's all this?"

"Just doing a little research. Since I'm going with you next week, I figured I should learn something about raptors."

He smiled. "That's nice, Jenny."

She scooted closer. "What sort of questions do you think the children will ask?"

"I don't know. I've never worked with kids before. The volunteers who normally go to the schools aren't available this time." He removed his hat and set it on an end table. "I'm not really sure what to expect. You know how unpredictable kids are."

He sounded a little nervous, she thought. But since he was used to an adult audience, she could understand his concern. "I'll be there to help you."

"Thanks. I appreciate that. The other volunteers told me to keep things fairly simple—the kids are only third graders."

"I thought it was the whole school." She had envisioned an auditorium-type presentation.

"No. The third-grade teachers contacted the center. Their students are studying birds of prey in science right now, so it fits their curriculum."

"I'm sure the kids will be thrilled to see the birds up close," she said. "It will be their best science class. A live presentation beats book work any day."

"Yeah, I suppose it does. Speaking of books—" he motioned to the one on her lap "—are you enjoying your research?"

She nodded. "You can quiz me later. I concentrated on red-tailed hawks, since you're going to bring Hera."

"I might bring a couple of owls, too. I used to be kind of spooked by them, but I've learned to appreciate their beauty."

She tilted her head. "You were afraid of owls?"

"They're considered ghosts in my culture, spirits that come and go from the grave. But I took the scientific approach and made peace with them. I don't think they're evil anymore." He scrunched up his face. "Of course, that raspy screech barn owls make still gets to me sometimes."

Curious, she scanned a birds-of-prey pocket guide

and checked the index for "barn owl." She turned to the page and studied the odd-looking creature. Its flat white face and small eyes did make it seem rather ghostlike.

"Are all Native Americans wary of owls?" she asked.

"No. I've heard they bring luck to some tribes. But either way, owl medicine is strong. It's important to respect it. I always ask the owls for permission to touch them."

Jenny closed the book, fascinated by Hawk's spiritual logic. In spite of the adjustment he'd made, he was still a taboo-conscious Apache.

He got to his feet. "I guess I should go home and get cleaned up." Reaching for his hat, he asked, "What do you want to do about dinner?"

"I already made a pot of spaghetti. We just have to reheat it and throw a salad together. Maybe some garlic bread." She took in his saddle-worn appearance. "You can bathe here, Hawk. You're welcome to use my shower." Something he'd yet to do.

"I'll have to bring some clothes over."

"That's fine." He could bring a whole closetful if he was so inclined.

"Okay." He turned to leave, then spun back around. "Are you going to join me in the shower, Jenny?"

A sensual shiver slid up her spine. Suddenly he looked downright edible.

A kiss beneath his collar, she thought. A slow lift of his shirt, a gentle nibble down his stomach. "Only if you let me undress you."

An eager smile tilted his lips. "I'll be back as soon as I can."

Ten minutes later he returned with an overnight bag and Muddy in tow. The dog ran to Jenny, and she picked him up for a quick nuzzle.

"I think I just lost my woman," Hawk said as Muddy snuggled into her arms.

She lifted her gaze and smiled at the man who'd captured her heart. "You'll never lose me." Releasing the puppy, she went to her lover.

Silently they entered the bathroom and closed the door. He placed his shaving kit on the counter and removed his boots.

When he turned to look at her, they both went a little crazy. She reached for him, and he backed her against the wall. As their tongues mated, she moaned and rubbed against him. He was already aroused. She could feel the hardness beneath his fly.

Reaching up, she unbuttoned his shirt and tossed it on the floor. Next she worked his zipper, tugged on his jeans and kissed her way down his body.

He tasted like salt and sexy man. His stomach muscles quivered, and the tip of his arousal, silky and warm, brushed her lips.

Working her way back up, she found his mouth. He undressed her then, peeling off her clothes and scattering them on top of his.

When they were both naked, he caressed her cheek. "I love you, Jenny."

Steeped in emotion, she caught her breath. "I love you, too."

He reached into his shaving kit and plucked out a condom. "I think we're going to need this."

She frowned, hoping for more, so much more. "Do we have to use it?"

For a moment he only stared. He twisted the packet between his thumb and forefinger. The foil seemed to wink as it caught the overhead light. "It's called safe sex, honey."

"But I want to feel you inside me." Slipping her hand between their bodies, she stroked him with a feather-light touch. "Just you."

A rough sound escaped his throat. "We can't make a baby, Jenny."

Why not? she wanted to ask. If we love each other, why can't we create a child? Desperate to hold him, to cling to her fantasy, she put her arms around him.

He pressed his forehead to hers. "It's risky, but I can pull out before I…"

"Climax," she whispered, wishing he was willing to spill inside her.

"Yes," he whispered back, his voice crackling with a desire so intense she could see it in his eyes.

He coaxed her into the shower and turned on the faucet. Water flowed, as smooth as a spring rain.

They caressed each other with slick, soapy hands. He washed her breasts, her belly, the V between her legs. She lathered his chest, his stomach, his jutting arousal.

Taking turns, they tasted each other, feeding on need, on passion, on the intimacy of love. And when he entered her, he thrust deep, so deep, she imagined him stroking her womb.

Their gazes locked, their hearts pounded. Steam rose, and pressure built in her loins, nearly triggering a release in his. She climaxed, and he drove himself even deeper, but only for one soul-shattering second.

Convulsing, he withdrew, then spent his seed, splashing milky warmth onto Jenny's skin. A moment later the rush of water from the shower rinsed it all away.

On Friday afternoon Jenny wandered into a guest room at the Lone Star Country Club to assess her work.

The four-poster bed, with its traditional curves and strong solid lines, drove the room. Limestone walls, novelty lamps and leather-fringed pillows added eclectic touches.

It was perfect, she thought, just the right blend of warm, woodsy antiques and bright, modern accents.

Pleased, she smiled. This was her reward—the completed project and the sense of pride that came with it.

"It's magnificent. You did a brilliant job."

She turned to find Hawk's father standing in the doorway. Her voice stumbled. "Th-thank you."

They gazed at each other until Archy cleared his throat. "I apologize if this is awkward, Jenny, but I need to speak to you. Privately, if I may."

She tried not to fumble again, to lose her composure. She still had mixed feelings about Archy. She knew he cared about her, yet he'd wounded Hawk so deeply she could feel her lover's pain.

"Come in," she said, knowing she had little choice.

He moved forward, his gait strong, purposeful. He didn't move as fluidly as Hawk, but not for the first time the similarity between the two struck her.

Although Jenny's pulse hammered, she tried to appear less affected than she felt. She closed the door. It seemed odd to host a private meeting in a room that didn't belong to her, but Archy had chosen the setting.

They sat across from each other at a small, hand-painted table. Jenny scooted in her chair, and Archy placed his hands on the tabletop.

"Have things progressed with you and Hawk?" he asked.

She drew a breath. "Progressed?"

"Are you in love with him?"

"Yes," she responded.

"And he's in love with you, isn't he?"

She nodded, unsure where this conversation was leading. Squaring her shoulders, she exhaled. "I don't see where this concerns you."

"I'm his father, Jenny."

"In name only," she countered.

"Yes, that's true." His expression troubled, he traced a pattern on the table, and when he looked up, his blue eyes turned soft. "Tell me about him. Tell me what he's like."

"He's amazing," she said, wondering how she was supposed to describe the man she loved to the father who'd shunned him. "He's kind and caring, but he's strong, too. And spiritual," she added. "He has this ability, this gentle sort of power—he can actually feel my emotions.''

"His mother was like that. Sometimes she knew what I was thinking. Or she could predict what I was going to do. Rain Dancer was stunning, more beautiful than you can imagine.''

"Why did you hurt her?'' Jenny asked. ''Why did you sleep with her and then refuse to acknowledge her child?''

He heaved a sigh. ''Because I was still in love with my wife. I know that sounds crazy, but I thought Kate was having an affair, and I needed someone to comfort me. Someone who understood my emotions, someone who wouldn't judge me.''

Jenny shook her head, disturbed by his reasoning. He'd used Hawk's mother to make himself feel better. ''You sound like an extremely selfish man.''

"I was. And I suppose I still am.'' He frowned, a deep crevice forming between his brows. His face was marked with sun-burnished lines. ''I'm not very good at relationships. But I'm trying to change.''

She snapped her fingers. ''Just like that? You're going to become an instant daddy?''

"No.'' He reached for her hand and held it. ''But I realize now how wrong I was. I denied Hawk's paternity because of Kate. I kept hoping she would come back to me someday, and I didn't think that was possible if I allowed Hawk to be part of my life.''

Rather than pull away, Jenny allowed him to hold her hand. ''And now?''

"And now it's time to do the right thing. To apologize to my son, to tell him the truth. Every detail he's willing to hear.''

"What about Kate?" she asked.

"I'm trying to make amends with her, too. I want to win my wife back."

"How does she feel about Hawk?"

He sighed. "She empathizes with his pain, and she thinks he deserves better. She doesn't blame him for my mistakes. And she doesn't believe all the nasty gossip about him. She doesn't think he's the monster this town makes him out to be."

Silent, Jenny heard the raw emotion creeping into Archy's voice.

"I remember the first time I saw him. He was five years old, this handsome little boy with coal-black hair and dark eyes. He looked at me with such wonder. With such hope."

She drew her hand back. "You broke his heart that day."

"I know. But believe it or not, I didn't deny him completely. I went to see my attorney afterward and set up a trust fund for Hawk. But I didn't tell anyone, not Rain Dancer and certainly not Kate. It was my secret, my cowardly way of claiming him."

"I don't understand. If there's a trust fund, where is it? And why doesn't Hawk know about it?"

"It was supposed to be granted in the event of my death. Or at least, that was the original stipulation. But I want him to have it now."

Suddenly her heart ached for the father and the son. "You can't buy his love, Archy."

"That's not what I'm trying to do. Please," he implored, "I need your help, Jenny. I need you to convince Hawk to give me a chance. I've hurt him badly, and I'm trying to mend the destruction. The hole I left inside him."

She wanted to see that hole mended, too. She wanted Hawk to heal from the scars Archy had inflicted.

"Will you mediate?" he asked. "Will you help me reach my son?"

"Yes," she said softly, realizing it was the right thing to do, the only thing she could to do. "I will."

"Thank you."

She nodded, hoping Hawk would understand why she'd chosen to help Archy.

Fourteen

"I can't believe that son of a bitch asked you to mediate. He had no right to involve you."

Jenny gazed at Hawk. They sat outside on his porch steps, discussing her unexpected visit from Archy. "He wants to get to know you. He wants to apologize."

"Yeah, right. He wants to prove to his ex-wife how noble he's suddenly become. He flat out admitted to you that he was trying to make amends with her."

"I don't think that's what this is about. Archy seems sincere. He seems truly sorry for what he's done to you."

"Bull." Hawk jumped up and descended the stairs. Turning, he faced Jenny, his expression hard. When he squinted, tiny lines fanned out at the corners of his eyes, making him look a bit like his father. Behind him the sun was setting, melting in a hazy blue sky. The wind blew, shifting dry, desert-type air, stirring the leaves on the trees.

"What about the trust fund?" she asked.

"I don't give a damn about his money. He's treated me like a leper all these years and I'm supposed to be impressed by a trust fund?"

She lifted her chin to look up at him. "No, of course not. But I saw the remorse in his eyes and I heard him talk about the past. The trust fund was his way of claiming you, of caring.''

"How can you say that? How can you side with him?''

"I'm not siding with him. I just want to see you stop hurting. You need this, Hawk. You need to make some sort of peace with your father.''

He flexed his fingers, the veins in his hands tensing. His hair blew in the breeze, and the talons in his ears spun. He stood tall and tough and rebellious.

"I don't want to make peace with him. And I'm not hurting anymore. I could care less about Archy.''

That wasn't true, she thought. Hawk hurt every day of his life. His father had crushed the hopeful child he had once been, and that little boy was still buried somewhere deep within.

"It isn't fair,'' he said. "I finally find a woman who loves me, and my father convinces her that he's some sort of hero. Big, billionaire Archy, taking pity on his bastard son.''

"Oh, Hawk.'' Couldn't he see how the pain was destroying him? "I don't think your father is a hero. He's a selfish, self-righteous man, but he's trying to change. He's reaching out to the people he hurt.''

"Then tell him to reach out to my mother. He used her and then tossed her aside. Am I supposed to forgive him for that?''

"I don't know,'' Jenny said honestly. "But Archy talked about Rain Dancer. He said she understood his emotions. And you know that must be true. You told me that your mother believed he would come forward someday and give you his heart. Think about that, Hawk. Just think about it.''

He trapped her gaze, his eyes dark and intense. "I

have thought about it, but I know damn well Archy is doing this because of Kate. Denying that I was his son didn't work with her, so now he's trying the humble approach. And you're falling for it, too. Do you know how that makes me feel? The sense of betrayal?"

She wanted to cry, to draw her knees to her chest and weep. He didn't understand how much she loved him, how much she hurt for him. "I'm not betraying you."

"Then let it go. Drop it. Let me hate my father. Let me curse the Wainwright name."

"But it's your name. It's part of who you are." And it would be part of her if they ever married, a name their children would bear.

"That's right. And I'm keeping it just to defy Archy. My mother thought it legitimized my birth, but it didn't. And it never will."

She blinked back the tears she wouldn't let herself cry. "Do we have a future, Hawk?"

Stunned by the question, he frowned. "Of course we do. Why would you ask me something like that?"

She chewed her bottom lip, gnawing nervously. "Because lately I've been worried about it."

He sat next to her, thinking how vulnerable she looked in her oversize sweater and girlish ponytail, loose strands of hair falling from the ribbon-wrapped confinement. "What did I do to give you the impression that we didn't have a future?"

Avoiding his gaze, she glanced down at her hands. "You don't want to have a baby with me."

At a loss, he tilted her chin so he could see her eyes, those bluer-than-blue eyes. "I'd love to have a baby with you, just not now."

"Why not now?"

"Because we're not married, and there's no way I'm going to produce an illegitimate child." He would never do what his father had done.

She held his gaze. "Your children will be Wainwrights. They'll be Archy's grandchildren."

His shoulders tensed. "And that's a reason for me to allow the guy into my life?"

"Yes." She studied his posture, the taut, unyielding muscles. "I'm aware that you weren't originally planning on having children, and I know why. You were worried they would be scorned for just being yours."

She was right, he thought. He hadn't considered raising a family until he'd fallen in love with her. Now he had to face the dilemma she spoke of. No matter what, he would always be the illegitimate Wainwright, and his children would carry his curse. They'd grow up in the shadow of the recognized Wainrights. "I'll cross that bridge when I come to it."

"I know how difficult this is for you," she said. "I'm still struggling with my emotions, too. I haven't been to a support group, but I have every intention of going." Her breath hitched, a sound barely audible above the menacing wind. "But no matter how uncomfortable I am about it, I don't have a choice. I know it's the right thing to do."

Sensing where this was leading, he shook his head. "My situation is different from yours. Archy isn't my support group. He isn't part of a healing process."

"Yes, he is."

"No, he isn't." Why didn't she understand? Why

couldn't she see that Archy was coming between them?

"Can't you take a few days to think about it?" she asked.

"No, I can't." Because the odds were in Archy's favor. He wouldn't help his father win back his ex-wife. And he wouldn't let bygones be bygones. His hatred ran far too deep.

She skimmed her fingers over his cheek, making him ache inside. "If you won't do this for yourself, then do it for me. For us. For the children we're going to have."

Dear God. He struggled to find the words, a way to make her understand how he felt. "I'd do anything for you. *Anything.* I'd give my life if it meant saving yours, but I don't think you have a right to ask this of me."

"Yes, I do," she said, her voice broken. "I have a right to help you heal."

Suddenly desperate, he captured her hand and pressed it against his heart. "Let's go away from here. Let's start over someplace new." A place where Archy didn't exist. A place where the Wainwright name didn't matter. "We can get married, Jenny. And have a baby." A child with his dark skin and her tender smile, a child who would seal their union. "There's no reason for us to stay in Mission Creek. You're almost done decorating the rooms at the country club, and I can do business in some other equestrian town."

She splayed her fingers across his chest, her eyes misting. "I've wanted so badly to hear you say those words, to propose to me. But I can't marry you, not if we have to run away to do it. I'm tired of running, of feeling like a criminal. Leaving Mission Creek won't give us a fresh start, not if you're hiding from your past.''

It hurt to breathe, he thought. To draw air into his lungs, to feel his heart beating against her hand. She'd just turned down his proposal, the opportunity to start a new life together, to live somewhere else.

''Go home, Jenny,'' he said, fending off the pain, the razor-sharp slashes of betrayal. ''There's no point in continuing this conversation.'' She'd chosen his father over him. Archy had finally won. He'd managed to take Jenny away and leave Hawk with nothing again.

Jenny stared at her reflection in the bathroom mirror. Swollen eyes gazed back at her. She hadn't slept well. She'd tossed and turned half the night, thinking about Hawk and crying into her pillow. Was their relationship over? He'd told her to go home yesterday and that was last he'd spoken to her.

She added another dab of concealer, attempting to camouflage the evidence of tears. Finally she gave up on her makeup and got dressed, slipping on a simple beige pantsuit and a pair of low-heeled pumps.

The doorbell rang, and her pulse jumped. She took a deep breath and went to the door, praying Hawk was on the other side—to tell her how much he loved her, to agree that their future was more important than clinging to the bitterness of his past.

Please, she thought. Please be him.

''Hello, dear.''

Hope, along with her heart, deflated. Mrs. Pritchett stood on the porch, wearing a floral-printed dress and carrying a patent-leather pocketbook, a relic of the Eisenhower era.

Jenny summoned a polite smile. "You look nice," she said, deciding the outfit was an improvement over the dowdy housecoats.

"Thank you." Mrs. Pritchett turned and motioned to blue sedan parked on the curb. A young woman sat behind the wheel. "I'm going shopping with my niece. She's expecting a baby in June, and I'm buying her a crib."

A pang of envy constricted Jenny's chest. She didn't want to think about babies. Hawk's offer to father her children had been hasty at best, an impulsive proposal on the heels of panic. Run away and get married to avoid Archy, to avoid taking pride in the Wainwright name.

"Are you all right, dear?"

"What? Oh, yes, I'm fine."

The older woman pursed her lips. Her hair, coiffed into stiff curls, crowned her head in a thinning, gray bubble.

"I better get down to business," she said. "I don't want to worry you, but last night I happened to notice a curious vehicle in the neighborhood." She clutched her purse a little more tightly. "It was moving rather slowly, especially in front of your house. Now, it could have been someone searching for an address, but I thought it best to warn you."

Jenny pulse pounded. "Did you see the driver?" she asked, telling herself to remain calm, to not jump to conclusions.

"Not clearly, no. It was dark, so I couldn't tell if it was a man or a woman. But just so you know, it was a white SUV. I'm not sure about the make or model. They all look alike to me."

"Thank you. I'll keep my eye out."

"If I see it again, I'll try to get the license number. One can't be too careful." With that, Mrs. Pritchett reached out and patted Jenny's hand. "I better go. My niece is waiting."

Jenny watched the older woman climb into the sedan, then went back into her house, wondering about the mysterious SUV.

She didn't contemplate the situation for long. Within five minutes the doorbell pealed again.

And this time she found Hawk standing on her porch. Suddenly weak-kneed, she clutched the door handle for support.

"I hope I'm not disturbing you," he said.

"No. Of course not. Would you like to come in?"

He shook his head. "I'm on my way to work, and I'm running a little late."

Quite a bit late, she realized, checking her watch. He normally left for the barn long before this hour. She shouldn't have expected him in the first place, and now that he was here, she didn't know what to say.

"I was waiting for a report from Randall, and I couldn't concentrate until I heard from him," Hawk explained. "I'm still worried about you, Jenny."

Still worried? What did that mean? she wondered. That even though they were no longer lovers, he still cared? "What did Randall say?"

"Roy left for Las Vegas five days ago."

"Looking for me?"

"Randall doesn't think so. Roy is registered at a conference on the strip, so this appears to be an extended business trip. He isn't scheduled to return to Salt Lake City for another week."

Then the white SUV wasn't worth mentioning, she

thought. Or worth worrying about. "Thank you for the information. It helps to know where Roy is."

Hawk nodded, and Jenny continued to grasp the door handle, not trusting herself to let go. She longed to touch him, to hold him, to accept his impulsive proposal and become his runaway bride. But as much as she loved him, she knew that wasn't the answer.

He studied her from beneath the brim of his hat, his eyes barely visible. "Where are you going? You look like you're dressed for a meeting."

"I..." She hesitated, apprehensive to admit the truth. "I have an appointment at the club."

He lifted his hat a notch, revealing dark and troubled irises. "With Archy?"

"Yes. He asked me to lunch. He's anxious to know what happened."

"And what are you going to tell him?"

That I've lost you, she thought, her heart climbing to her throat. "That you're not interested in hearing what he has to say."

Hawk glanced away, then looked back at her, and for a short time they stared at each other, a lull of quiet stretching between them. Once again she longed to touch him, to lean into him and breathe in his scent. She'd missed sleeping in his arms last night, closing her eyes and curling against his warm body.

"What about Tuesday?" he asked, breaking the silence.

She blinked. "Tuesday?"

"Are you still going to assist me at the elementary school? Or do you want to cancel?"

With everything else going on, she'd forgotten about the third-grade science class. "I'd still like to go. If that isn't a problem for you."

"It isn't," he responded, his voice somehow gentle yet rough. "I could use the help."

Once again they stared at each other.

She continued to clutch the door handle, her palm numb, her fingers frozen. "I guess I'll see you on Tuesday, then."

"Okay." He lifted his hand as if he meant to touch her, then jammed it into his pocket and took a step back.

When he said goodbye and walked away, she fought the urge to cry.

Hours later Jenny sat across from Archy at the Yellow Rose Café. As usual she'd requested a table near the window so she could see the garden.

"I'm sorry," Archy said as their lunch neared its end. "I never meant to come between you and Hawk. Damn it, why does he have to be so stubborn?"

She toyed with her spoon. "You're stubborn, too. After all, it took you thirty-three years to acknowledge him."

"All right, so he inherited that trait from me. But he shouldn't be so bull-headed with the woman he loves." He motioned to her bowl. "Finish your soup. You're going to waste away."

"I'm not very hungry." Every time she took a mouthful, her stomach cramped. "Food doesn't agree with me when I'm stressed."

"Me, neither." Archy glanced at his half-eaten burger, then checked his watch. "It's time for me to go."

She knew he had another meeting. "That's all right. We've said everything there is to say."

"Yes, I suppose we have."

He rose, and she stood to hug him, needing to cling to someone. He felt big and strong, reminding her of her own father, long since passed away. She didn't remember much about him. She'd been so young when he died.

"I miss my dad," she said suddenly.

Archy stepped back and tilted her chin. Blinking furiously, she did her damnedest not to cry.

"I wouldn't exactly win father of the year," he said. "But you're welcome to call me anytime."

"Thank you." Flustered by the concern in his eyes, she smoothed his lapels. "Now, you better go or you'll be late for your meeting."

As Archy signed for the bill and left the café, Jenny resumed her seat and stared out the window, hoping to calm her emotions.

As always, the garden flourished. Flowers bloomed in the sun, the petals basking in its shining rays.

"Jenny?"

She turned and saw Daisy. "Mr. Wainwright told me to bring you a slice of apple pie. Not for now, but for later," he said. She set the plastic container on the table. "Just in case you get your appetite back."

"Thank you."

As usual Daisy's smile belied the sadness in her eyes. And today Jenny understood it. She smiled, too, even though her heart was breaking.

Daisy moved to another table, refilling coffee. Jenny turned back to the window—and lost her breath.

Two glorious white doves lit upon the familiar rustic bench, looking as heavenly as angels. They were mates, she thought. Beautiful lovers. And they were sending her a message. But what? She stole a quick glance at Daisy, who disappeared into the kitchen.

Within the beat of a drum, the birds fanned their wings and soared away, leaving Jenny staring after them.

Too emotional to think clearly, she rose to her feet and exited the café, where she plowed straight into a hard, muscular body.

"I'm sorry. I—" Clutching the pie she'd nearly dropped, she glanced up at the man she'd bumped into and wanted to die a thousand deaths. She recognized him from the club. But he wasn't just any member. The young, handsome millionaire was blind. Not born blind, she recalled. He'd lost his sight in some sort of accident.

"I'm sorry," she tried again. "I didn't see you."

"I didn't see you, either," he responded, his lips twisting in a wry smile.

Mortified, Jenny winced. Had she actually prompted him to say that?

"Who are you?" he asked.

"Jenny Taylor. I'm the interior designer who worked on the renovations at the club."

He extended his hand. "Nice to meet you. I'm Luke Callaghan."

Should she offer to guide him to the café? She'd noticed another man standing nearby, but he seemed to be holding back, allowing Luke to decide what came next.

He released her hand. "Do you know Daisy Parker?"

Curious now, she tilted her head. "Yes. I just saw her."

"Would you mind asking her to come out here? But don't mention my name. I'd like to surprise her."

Jenny returned to the café and found Daisy just getting ready to go on her break. She wondered if Luke had timed his visit.

The instant Daisy saw Luke, she gasped. Luke seemed to sense the waitress's presence, and Jenny felt a shift of air. A softly scented breeze swirled around them, sending Daisy's hair spilling around her face.

The wind crackled with heat, with tension, with the kind of energy that drew lovers into its spell.

Jenny thought about the doves, certain Luke Callaghan was the reason they had appeared.

Leaving Luke and Daisy alone, she passed Luke's friend. He, too, had moved a distance away, giving the couple privacy.

Jenny wanted to glance back, to hear their voices, to solve their mystery, but she continued to her car, instead. And when she got behind the wheel, she didn't notice the white SUV or the man who'd been watching her.

Luke moved closer to Daisy. He could hear her anxious breaths. Was she the woman from the Saddlebag? The beautiful blonde he'd made love to? He conjured up an image of her in his mind: her sleek, tanned skin, her exotic eyes, those long, shapely legs wrapped around his waist.

Lifting his hand, he connected with her hair and felt it slide through his fingers. Steeped in her scent, in a fragrance he remembered, he pulled her tight against him.

"You feel the same," he whispered.

Her attempt to pull away was halfhearted at best. "I don't know what you're talking about. You must have me confused with someone else."

Ignoring her denial, he brushed her mouth with his. "I wonder if you taste the same."

"I—"

He stilled her words with a kiss. His tongue stroked hers, slow and easy at first, then deeper, stronger. With an unconscious shiver, she gripped his shoulders and kissed him back, willing, wanting, eager to be touched.

And then he knew, damn it, he knew. She was the same woman. The unnamed woman who had made love with him.

And given him a child.

She pulled back, breaking the connection. "I have to go."

"No." Luke tried to keep her, to grab her hand, but he lost her. He heard her hasty retreat, her footsteps sounding on the cement walk, then disappearing into the building.

"I'll find out what she's hiding," he said, cursing to himself. Sooner or later he would uncover her secret.

While Luke stood in the rioting wind, Daisy rushed through the café, making her way to the bathroom.

Leaning against the sink, she touched a finger to her lips. She could still taste him, the rich, masculine flavor. Luke, she thought. Her Luke. She hadn't meant to kiss him, but when his tongue had coaxed hers, she'd lost control.

She turned and gazed at herself in the mirror.

She couldn't tell Luke who she was. Once the FBI made the bust and the main "family" members were arrested and charged, she could emerge from hiding. But until then she had to keep silent.

Feeling vulnerable and alone, she sighed. She couldn't tell anyone who she was, not even her father or her brother—the only two people in the world who were probably still mourning her death.

The Mercado home sat on a hill overlooking the town of Mission Creek. A state-of-the-art alarm system and strategically placed security cameras kept intruders at bay.

But that didn't ease Johnny Mercado's mind. He couldn't stop thinking about the kidnapped child.

Whose little girl was she? he asked himself. And why would mafia boss Frank Del Brio take her?

Johnny had been spying on Frank, a man who was once engaged to Johnny's daughter, Haley.

But Haley was dead. She'd gone to a watery grave years ago.

Or had she?

Was it possible Haley was still alive? Frank kept insisting she was.

Johnny stared out the window. Trees surrounded the estate, giving the brick structure a privacy, a seclusion, a loneliness Johnny could no longer bear.

He thought about Haley again. And the child, the little girl Frank had taken.

Frank was a cold, calculating man—a man who would do anything to protect his future with "the family."

Johnny smoothed his gray hair with a trembling hand. How would Frank react if Haley had deceived the mob? If she wasn't really dead? If she'd given birth to a secret baby?

Was that possible? Did the kidnapped child belong to Haley?

Of course it was possible. Why else would Frank want the child? He could force Haley out of hiding by threatening to hurt the baby.

Johnny sank into a chair and dimmed the light. If that little girl was Haley's daughter, then she was also his grandchild, his flesh and blood.

Damn it, Haley. Where are you? And who are you? What identity are you living under?

Sick at heart, Johnny dropped his head into his hands. What would it be like to be an average guy? To not be tied to the mob?

His daughter was living a lie somewhere, and Frank was keeping his granddaughter in a small, unassuming rental in Goldenrod. Johnny knew because he'd seen Frank's girlfriend with the child.

Johnny lifted his head, certain now of what he must do. He had to rescue the child, get her back. But the mission must be carefully planned. Secretly planned. He couldn't accomplish this overnight, and he couldn't tell anyone.

Ricky entered the den, giving Johnny a start. He sat forward in the leather recliner and met his son's curious gaze.

"Pop?" Ricky frowned. "What are you doing sitting in the dark?"

"Just resting my eyes." Squinting, he studied Haley's brother. If he confided in Ricky, he could put the young man in danger.

Ricky dragged a hand through his hair. He'd recently returned from Central America, but he wasn't sure if it felt good to be home. He'd stopped by his dad's house to visit him, but the older man seemed distant and preoccupied.

Well, hell. Ricky had problems of his own. Mob boss Frank Del Brio was a loose cannon, one that could explode anytime. Ricky didn't trust him. The other man kept going on and on about Haley still being alive, which made Ricky wonder if Frank knew where she was.

But Ricky had to curb his anger and play his role in the next smuggling operation. In a few weeks the Mayan artifacts would arrive, and Ricky would be there, feigning loyalty to Frank.

He glanced at his dad and cursed the life they'd been leading. Maybe he ought to go back into the military, back to a world that felt solid and honorable. Back to a world that didn't include Mission Creek or the distress it seemed to breed.

Fifteen

On Tuesday morning Hawk stood beside Jenny in the confinement of a mews, the air between them sparked with emotion. He missed her desperately, but he didn't know how to come to terms with what she'd asked him to do.

"We're supposed to be there by one o'clock," she said. "But I'm not prepared."

"Sure you are. You read all those books." And in spite of her nervousness, he was counting on her to get him through his first elementary-school presentation.

"But I didn't study this species."

"That's okay." He sensed her discomfort had more to do with him than the owls. "I can tell you what you need to know."

She removed a notebook and pen from her purse, waiting to take notes, to keep her mind and her hands busy.

"Saw-whet owls aren't native to this region, but we get raptors from all over," he told her.

She studied the birds, her expression rather sweet, and he felt his heart clench. She looked so pretty, with her gold-streaked hair and sky-blue eyes.

"The kids are going to love seeing one up close," she said, her mood lighter. "They're so cute."

Hawk gave the little creatures another gander. Saw-whets were tuftless owls about the size of a robin. Their heads looked too big for their bodies, and their eyes shone big and yellow. He supposed they were cute, in an odd sort of way. "They're not the smallest owl in North America, but they're close."

She poised her pen. "How did they get their name?"

"When they're alarmed, they make a sound that resembles a saw being whetted."

"That makes sense." She jotted down the information, even though it wasn't something she was likely to forget.

"But even so," he went on, "they're not a noisy bird. They only vocalize during breeding season. They're silent at other times of the year."

She glanced up. "Is this breeding season?"

He held her gaze. "Yes."

"Do they mate for life?"

"No. But their courtship is based on a song. A male will fly above a female and sing, and once he attracts her, he lands and starts inching toward her."

"Oh." Visibly uncomfortable, Jenny chewed her lip. "Maybe we shouldn't talk about their mating practice to the kids."

"Then why did you ask?"

"I just wondered, I guess."

Because of us, Hawk thought. When they made love, they mated like birds, flying in courtship circles and landing in each other's arms.

She glanced at the owls, then back at him. He had the notion to move closer, to run his hands through her hair, to feel what he was missing.

How am I going to live without her? he asked himself. He'd found his mate, the match for his soul, yet he was letting her go.

Because of his grudge against Archy.

Suddenly that seemed wrong. So incredibly wrong. He'd chosen hatred over love, detachment over unity. All of his adult life he'd longed to have a woman by his side, but he'd become a lone wolf, instead, a man with a desolate spirit.

"I don't want to lose you," he said.

"I don't want to lose you, either." Her voice broke on a sigh. "But if we run away, it won't work."

"I know." And because he knew, his hands began to quake.

She stepped forward, and when she burrowed against his chest, he stroked her back. This overwhelmed him, he thought. This feeling, this gentle power she held over him.

"I'd die for you, Jenny."

She lifted her head. He'd told her that before, but suddenly it felt like a possibility, something she could imagine happening. "Don't say that."

"But it's true." He touched her cheek, his fingers cool against her skin.

She kept her eyes on his. "If you died, I wouldn't want to live."

They both fell silent then, the intensity of their words drawing out the moment. Jenny clung to him, struggling to push away the flicker of fear.

"If keeping you means giving Archy a chance, then I'll do it," he said. "I'll do whatever it takes."

"Thank you," she whispered, realizing he was sacrificing his pride for her, the years he'd spent building a wall around his pain. "I'll go with you to your dad's house if you want me to."

"No." He shook his head. "This is something I need to do alone."

"When will you go?"

"Tonight." He let out a choppy breath. "The sooner the better. I don't want this hovering over our heads."

"Are you going to be able to forgive him, Hawk?"

"I don't know," he said, making a solemn vow. "But I promise to try."

Jenny gazed at the man she loved, knowing this should be the happiest moment of her life, yet she couldn't seem to shake the unsettling quiver of fear. The reality that he would truly die for her.

The evening brought bouts of silence. Jenny sat on the edge of Hawk's bed, watching him dress. She'd called Archy a few hours before and told him to expect his son. And now the time neared.

She knew Hawk was nervous. She could see the restless shift of his muscles, the tense roll of his shoulders.

She was nervous, too. But not because of Hawk's meeting with Archy. Her anxiety stemmed from something else, from something she couldn't quite name.

Hawk finished buttoning his shirt and tucking the tails into his pants. After zipping his fly, he reached for his boots.

Jenny fisted the quilt, clutching the fabric. Why was she so nervous? So fretful?

Because they'd talked about death, she realized. And they'd done it in front of the owls, the creatures that represented ghosts in the Chiricahua culture.

What a time to be superstitious. Hawk needed her

support, not her trumped-up fear. If he wasn't afraid of the Apache myth connected to owls, then she shouldn't be, either.

"What's the matter, Jenny?"

She released her hold on the quilt. "Nothing."

"You seem worried."

She was. Worried that he would die, that she would lose him tonight. Oh, God. What an awful thing to think, to feel.

He sat beside her. "Jenny?" he pressed.

"I'm fine." She reached up to stroke his face. She couldn't burden him with the craziness going on in her head. She couldn't stop him from leaving the house, from seeing his father. This was part of his healing, the cleansing of his spirit.

Maybe that was the owls' message, she thought. Hawk was being reborn tonight. Not dying, but being reborn.

"I love you," she said.

"I love you, too." He kissed her, softly, gently, with a vow so tender, so intense, she could feel his soul melding with hers.

He brushed a lock of hair from her cheek, and she met the magic in his eyes. For a quiet moment they gazed at each other, their hearts filled with enchantment. And then he dropped his hand.

"It's time for me to go."

He stood and sorted through his belongings on the dresser. He stuffed his wallet into his back pocket and frowned at his cell phone.

"The damn thing is dead again. This has been happening for the past two days. It won't hold a charge."

"You can borrow mine."

"That's okay. I can use Archy's phone if I need to

call.'' He paused, blowing out a breath. ''I just want to get this over with.''

Jenny rose from the bed. ''What you're doing means so much to me.''

''I know.'' He drew her into his arms, and they held each other.

She inhaled his scent, the smell of sage clinging to his skin. He'd purified himself in a lone smudging ceremony, she realized. He'd prepared himself for the night ahead.

He stepped back. ''Will you take Muddy to your place while I'm gone?''

She nodded and glanced at the puppy. He'd fallen asleep on a pile of Hawk's discarded clothes. ''I'll get him now.''

With Jenny carrying the dog, she and Hawk exited his house and walked to hers.

Once they were on the porch, Hawk unlocked her door with his key. ''I'll see you later.''

''Okay.'' She brushed his lips with a kiss, and they stared at each other, caught once again in the glitter of enchantment.

''Marry me,'' he whispered.

''I will,'' she whispered back.

Missing him already, she stood at the door and watched him depart. He cut across the lawn and disappeared from view.

She went inside and set Muddy on the floor. The dog yawned, then scratched his ear. A moment later he went to the kitchen and stood at the back door, telling her his bladder was full.

She let him out and promised to come back for him in a few minutes. After removing her shoes, she headed to the bedroom, turned on the light—and stumbled straight into a nightmare.

"Scream and I'll shoot."

Oh, God. Dear God. Panic raced through her veins, sending a clammy shiver up her spine.

Roy raised the gun in his hand. "Where's your lover? Where's the half-breed?"

Her limbs began to tremble.

I'd die for you, Jenny.

"He isn't here."

"But he's coming back, isn't he?"

"No…no. He isn't." Frantic, she glanced around the room, looking for something, anything to hit him with. "We broke up. I'm not seeing him any—"

"You cheating, lying bitch." Roy lunged, and then grabbed her by the neck, constricting her throat.

She struggled to free herself, trying desperately to shove him away. Enraged, he slammed the gun against the side of her head. A burst of pain exploded behind her eyes before she slid to the floor in an unconscious heap.

Hawk sat across from Archy in an elegant room at the Wainwright mansion, uneasy and tense. The housekeeper had brought him a beer, but he hadn't touched it.

"I'm here because of Jenny," he said.

"I know." Archy took a swig of his drink, and they gazed at each other.

The house seemed quiet, almost ghostly, and Hawk got an ominous feeling he couldn't quite explain. Maybe the mansion was haunted. With memories, he thought. Bad memories.

His father cleared his throat. "I'm sorry for calling

you a cocky bastard. At the barn that day," he clarified. "I was curious about you, and I couldn't think of another reason to stop by, so I figured I'd offer you some work."

Hawk didn't respond, so Archy continued, "I'm sorry for a lot of things I've done and said over the years. I've hurt so many people."

"You hurt my mother. That bothers me the most."

"I know this might sound odd after what I did to her, but Rain Dancer was my friend. She gave riding lessons at the club, and I used to spend a lot of time at the stable, chatting with her."

Hawk kept his expression blank, and Archy explained further.

"Once I began to suspect that Kate was cheating on me, I went to Rain Dancer. I needed someone to talk to, and she was always ready to listen, to be my friend." He glanced at his beer, twisted the bottle in his hand. "I knew she was attracted to me."

Hawk's back went stiff. "So you're saying my mother instigated the affair?"

"No, not at all." Archy rose. He walked to the fireplace, set his beer on the gilded mantel. The bottle looked out of place, sandwiched between two crystal candelabras. "I asked her to have coffee with me, and we ended up—" he paused, his voice quiet "—in bed that afternoon. I knew she was vulnerable to me, and I seduced her."

Hawk shifted in his seat, recalling bits and pieces his mother had told him. "She thought you were going to leave your wife for her."

"Yes, but that's because I continued the affair for several weeks, giving her the impression that my marriage was over. But then I got vengeful about Kate, and I hired a P.I. to follow her, to get pictures of her and her lover, photographs I could throw in her face.''

''And that's when you discovered there was no lover.''

His father nodded tightly.

Hawk's mouth went dry, and he finally took a quick swallow of the beer. ''Is this supposed to make me feel better?''

''No, but it's the truth. And you have the right to hear it.'' Archy frowned, and the lines around his eyes deepened. ''I'm sorry, son.''

Don't call me son, Hawk wanted to say, but he held his tongue, recalling his promise to Jenny.

''Although your mother was hurt, she seemed to understand. She knew how much I loved Kate. But that's because she felt the same way about Keith. She never really got over losing him.''

''Keith?'' Confused, Hawk shook his head. ''Who the hell is he?''

Archy resumed his seat. ''He was your mother's first lover. But his family didn't approve of her. She was Apache, and he came from a prestigious white family.''

''So what happened?''

''Keith and your mother became secret lovers, and she got pregnant.''

Everything inside Hawk went still. Very still. ''There was a child?''

''Yes, but she miscarried. She lost the baby soon after Keith was killed in a car accident. They loved each other very much. And in spite of his family's disapproval, Keith intended to marry her.''

''She never told me any of this.'' And it stunned him now. The Apache rarely spoke of those who had died, so he understood her silence. But why had she confided in Archy?

Then the answer hit him. "You reminded her of Keith, didn't you?"

"Yes. She left Oklahoma after he died. And when she came to Texas, she met me, a married man who resembled him."

Hawk wanted to cry, to mourn for Keith and his mother and the child they had lost.

Archy's voice turned raw. "Years later, when I'd heard that Rain Dancer had died in an accident, I thought about Keith. I realized that she'd gone to him. That they were finally together."

Hawk looked up, surprised by his father's emotion.

"Sometimes I used to think of you as Keith's son," the older man said. "If you had the same spirit as the baby your mother had lost, then somehow that made you his. But that was selfish of me, just a way to cover my shame."

"I'm not that child. We don't share the same spirit. That's not the Apache way."

"You're my son," Archy admitted. "With a spirit I helped create. And I've wronged you." His voice turned raw again, rough and shaky. "On the night my daughter, your sister, Rose, nearly died, I made a vow to right that wrong. At the hospital I looked at my other children, hoping to draw comfort from them, and I realized you were missing."

Hawk met his father's gaze. "I don't know what to say."

"Just say you'll try to forgive me. And accept the trust fund I established for you."

"I already promised Jenny I would try to forgive you, but the money—"

"Please. It's not a bribe. It's your birthright. It was my way of claiming you, even if I'd never told anyone but my attorney."

"But—"

"You can buy Jenny a house," Archy persisted. "A ranch. A place to raise horses and children. Lots of children," he added. "Little Wainwrights."

Hawk couldn't help but smile. "I think Jenny would like that."

"Then you'll accept the money?"

"I'll talk to Jenny about it."

Hawk stood, and Archy rose, as well. They shook hands, and the gesture felt right. Good and strong and solid.

"There's a spring ball coming up," Archy said. "I invited Jenny a while ago. At the time she wasn't interested, but if you escort her, I'll think she'll change her mind. Will you attend? Will you let me introduce you around as my son?"

A lump formed in Hawk's throat. "Yes," he responded, touched by the sincerity he saw in his father's eyes. "But for now, I just want to go home and be with my woman."

He said goodbye to Archy, anxious to tell Jenny that everything would be all right.

Jenny opened her eyes, and the room spun in a distorted blur. She lay on her side on the bed, her hands tied behind her back, her ankles bound, a gag pulled tightly around her mouth. She tried to move her wrists and realized they were attached to a bedpost.

She blinked and tried to focus. And then she saw him. Roy sat in a chair he must have dragged in from the dining room. He stared at her with a superior expression, the gun tucked in the waistband of his trousers.

"Glad you could join us," he said.

Us? A soft sound of horror escaped her lips, muffled by the gag. Did he mean him and the gun?

He moved the chair a little closer to the bed. "This wasn't part of my original plan. I came to Texas almost a week ago, intending to take you back home, to show you I still cared." He leaned in, his eyes narrowing into dark slits. "But you broke the rules. You cheated."

The room tilted again, pushing him off-kilter.

"I was going to forgive you for divorcing me, for running away, but now I can't." He stroked the handle of the gun, drawing her attention to it. "Not when you've been screwing another man."

Tears stung her eyes, and he smiled.

"I'm going to murder your lover. I'm taking my revenge."

A spear of nausea pierced her stomach, making her hot and then cold. Bone-chilling cold.

I'd die for you, Jenny.

No, she thought. No. Don't come back, Hawk. Don't come here.

"You turned me into a criminal, Jenny. I parked my car around back, waited for the right moment and jarred a window to get into your house. And now I have to kill someone." He bore his gaze into hers. "And it's all your fault."

The phone rang, sending her heart careering to her throat. Roy jumped up, and they both waited for the machine to answer it.

"Ms. Taylor," a masculine voice said. "It's Dusty

Randall. I just called the hotel in Las Vegas to verify Segal's whereabouts and discovered that he checked out of his room last Tuesday.'' After a slight pause he went on. ''I left a message on Hawk's home phone, but I was unable to reach his cell. I'll get back to both of you as soon as I have more information.''

As Randall left his number and hung up, Roy spun around, his face mottled in rage. ''Loverboy hired a P.I.? Someone to spy on me?''

Fighting another wave of nausea, she struggled to breathe, to keep herself from passing out again. If only she had paid closer attention to the white vehicle Mrs. Pritchett had seen. If only she had told Hawk.

''He deserves to die. That wife-stealing bastard deserves to die.'' Roy paced the room like a madman, mumbling to himself.

Oh, God. Dear God. She made a muffled sound, and the tears burning her eyes fell onto her cheeks. Roy stopped pacing and lifted his head. He began to rub his arms in harsh, scrubbing motions. ''It's too late for you to beg. I could never take you back.'' His features contorted; his mouth twisted around his words. ''I don't want you anymore, not with your bleached hair and slutty ways. You were a virgin on our wedding night, but he turned you into a tramp. Now you have to watch him bleed.''

I'd die for you, Jenny. I'd die for you.

The dizziness returned, slamming into her like a fist, stealing oxygen from her lungs. *Don't come here, Hawk. Go home first. Listen to Randall's message.*

Roy returned to the chair, his eyes glazed. ''Do you know how I found you, Jenny?''

She glanced at her ankles, at the rope he'd secured around them. He was too far away to kick, she thought. Even if she twisted her body, she couldn't reach him. There was nothing she could do to help Hawk, to incapacitate Roy.

"I was in Las Vegas, as you well know, and I met a man at the convention. His wife was an interior designer from Austin. It was such a coincidence." He rocked back, smiled a little. "One thing led to another, and I learned that a designer from Salt Lake City had gotten a big job she was after. That's right, baby. The Lone Star Country Club. You—"

The bedroom door opened and for a split second she saw Hawk. Saw the stunned horror in his eyes. He didn't know. He hadn't gone home first.

Roy grabbed his gun and leaped out of his chair. Hawk lunged, and the men collided.

Jenny's vision blurred again, fear gripping her heart. They looked like shadows, bouncing back and forth, struggling for control of the gun.

She focused on Hawk's shadow, on the breadth of his shoulders, on the flowing line of his hair, knowing she was going to pass out again.

Roy knocked Hawk to the floor, and Hawk pulled the other man down with him.

And as Jenny began to lose consciousness, the gun went off, the hollow blast reverberating in her ears.

Sixteen

The hospital room was quiet. The TV played without the volume, sitcom images flickering in the dim light.

Hawk sat beside the bed, where he'd been for hours, and watched Jenny sleep. She looked fragile, like a china doll, with pale skin and fluttering lashes.

Restless, she turned and moaned, the slight motion and soft sound filled with distress.

He reached for her hand to calm her, to let her know he was there.

"I love you," he whispered, his words blending gently into the night.

She moaned again and opened her eyes. Then she stared at him as if she was seeing a ghost.

"Oh, God." Her voice came out brokenly. "I'm dreaming again. I keep seeing you, but you're not real."

He raised their joined hands and brushed his lips across her fingers. "I'm real. I'm here. The doctor said you might be confused. You have a concussion."

"But I had this awful feeling that you were going to die. And then Roy showed up and told me he was going to kill you. When the gun went off—"

"It was a wild shot. It didn't hit anyone. Roy and I struggled. I got control of the gun and I knocked him out. Afterward I called the sheriff." But there had been one moment, he thought, one enraged moment when he'd considered aiming the gun at Roy's head and pulling the trigger, even though the other man had been unconscious. "The sheriff arrested him and an ambulance came for you."

Tears flooded her eyes. "You're really here. You're alive."

"Yes." He met her misty gaze. "I'm alive."

"Let me feel your heartbeat. Please, let me feel it."

Hawk left his chair and sat on the bed next to Jenny. He unbuttoned his shirt partway, and she put her head on his chest. While she listened to the beats, he stroked her hair.

"I wish you could stay here with me," she said.

Her hair slipped through his fingers, smooth and silky. She still looked fragile, but her cheeks had gained a pale wash of color. "I'll stay until you fall asleep for the night, and I'll come back first thing in the morning."

"My head hurts." She turned her face and pressed her lips against his chest.

"You'll feel better in a day or so." He'd been told what to expect, but seeing her like this pained him. It made him think about killing Roy again, about pulling that trigger. "Headaches, sleepiness. That's part of the concussion."

"I want to go home. I want to be with you."

"You'll be home soon." And until then, he would stay by her side as long as the hospital would allow. "I'll never let anyone hurt you again, Jenny. I promise." From now until eternity, he would keep her safe. "You're everything to me. You're my world." He loved her so much he ached inside.

She sighed against his chest, the flutter of air whispering over his skin. Lost in the feel of her, he closed his eyes, until a short while later when the door creaked.

Hawk opened his eyes and saw the sheriff—his half brother Justin—coming into the room.

They stared at each other for a second, two men who shared the Wainwright blood.

"I'm sorry," Justin said. "I didn't mean to interrupt. I just wanted to see how Jenny was doing."

At the mention of her name, she lifted her head. Hawk righted his shirt, and Justin pretended not to notice. Hawk couldn't help but wonder if Justin had a woman in his life. He'd heard that Justin had been married and divorced some years ago, but in truth he didn't know much about his older brother—the seemingly dedicated lawman who'd hauled Roy Segal away in cuffs just hours before.

"I'm going to be okay," Jenny said.

The sheriff moved farther into the room, the silver badge on his chest reflecting the dim light. Like a shield of honor, Hawk thought, wondering about Justin again. He had a rough-around-the-edges quality, but the smile he sent Jenny's way gentled his rugged features. Hawk could see that he put her at ease.

The lawman searched Jenny's gaze. "I'd like to get a statement from you when you're up to it."

"I'm still kind of groggy, but I remember everything Roy did to me. And everything he said he was going to do to Hawk." Leaning against the pillow, she smoothed the blanket. "I'll testify in court. I'll do whatever it takes to keep him behind bars."

"Good." Justin gave a solemn nod, and Hawk turned to study Jenny.

This was her strength, he thought. Her fight against Roy, her stand against years of abuse.

"I'll return tomorrow, and we can talk then." Justin glanced out the window at the darkness. "But for now I think you need to rest."

She agreed, and Hawk walked the sheriff out, promising Jenny he would be right back.

Hawk and Justin faced each other in the bright, sterile hallway. An orderly whisked by, and they remained silent for several long, awkward beats.

"Thanks for checking up on Jenny," Hawk said finally.

"No problem."

"What is Segal being charged with?"

The sheriff shifted his stance. "Attempted murder, assault with a deadly weapon, false imprisonment. He's going to do some serious time."

Hawk took a big breath. He would never forget the horrifying image of opening the bedroom door and seeing Jenny bound and gagged. "False imprisonment? Is that for tying Jenny up?"

Justin nodded. "I told Dad what happened, and he intends to call in a favor at the D.A.'s office. He'll make damn sure we get the best prosecutor on this case."

"I appreciate that." For the first time in his life, Hawk was grateful for the power the Wainwright name wielded.

"By the way," Justin said, "Dad wants to see Jenny."

"That's fine. He's welcome anytime." Hawk cleared his throat, realizing how odd his invitation sounded. After all the pain, the humiliation of being shunned, he was actually welcoming his father. "Did Archy tell you that we're trying to work things out?"

"Yes, he did." The other man sent him a steady

gaze, his eyes a deep shade of green. "I guess this means you and I will be getting to know each other, too."

"Yeah, I guess it does."

Justin extended his hand, and Hawk felt a strong sense of relief, recalling his childhood longing, the gut-wrenching years he'd prayed for acceptance, prayed to feel like his brother's equal.

As Justin headed to the elevator, Hawk went back into the room. Jenny reached out to him, and he went to her, holding her until she drifted into a safe, tranquil sleep.

A week later Hawk and Jenny shared the same bathroom, getting ready for the Lone Star Country Club's spring ball.

They were half-dressed, a man and woman in a domestic, intimate setting. Hawk wore only a pair of tuxedo pants, and Jenny, besides her bra and panties, a white-gold wedding ring.

They'd gotten married two days before in a private ceremony. They did it in the old way, the Chiricahua way, when a couple began their life together without ritual or formality; it seemed fitting for Jenny and Hawk. They'd been through too much to wait, to plan a fancy event that would keep them from being husband and wife for any longer than necessary.

The ring on her finger sparkled with a row of diamonds. Hawk sported a similar band. They considered the rings their only indulgence, a tradition they couldn't resist.

While Jenny applied blusher to her cheeks, Hawk combed his hair.

"Are you nervous?" she asked.

"A little," he responded.

She understood his anxiety. Tonight his father would introduce him to people who, in the past, had thought poorly of him.

Replacing her makeup brush in its container, she met his gaze in the mirror. "Is there anything I can do to help you relax?"

One eyebrow raised in a wicked slash of black. "Actually, Mrs. Wainwright, I think there is."

The color she'd just applied to her cheeks deepened. She turned to face him, and he lifted her onto the counter and scooted her to its edge.

Their eyes met and held. In the silence, they took pleasure in just looking at each other, in knowing moments like these were theirs to keep.

Jenny unhooked her bra and tossed it on the floor. As Hawk nuzzled her breasts, she slid her panties down and brought his hand between her legs.

But he had another idea, one that swept through her like a river, a current of pure need. He dropped to his knees, lifted her legs onto his shoulders and kissed between her thighs.

She bucked beneath his touch, and Hawk grasped her hips, holding her in place, setting a slow, sweet rhythm. He found her slick and warm. Smooth and wet.

He looked up at her, and she touched his face, caressing his cheek while he stoked the embers of her fire. He wanted her like this. Lost in the moment, in the feel of his mouth, his tongue.

Jenny arched her back, and he felt her body quiver, her breath rush out in a long, luxurious sigh.

She climaxed on a dream, on silk and sensation, rubbing sensuously against him. Tasting her release, he gave her everything—his heart, his soul, his very being.

But that wasn't enough. Not nearly enough. He wanted to give her more.

Anxious, Hawk came to his feet and unzipped his trousers. Sealing their union with a kiss, he entered her, joining their bodies in passion, in need, in the knowledge that they belonged to each other.

He thrust deep, moving in and out, heightening the feeling, the pleasure, the sexual beauty of being in love.

Blood swam in his head and flowed through his veins, making his loins throb with an ache he couldn't describe.

He caught their reflection in the mirror, and what he saw aroused him further. The slim line of her back, the crease of her bottom, her legs wrapped around his waist while he moved inside her.

Dropping his gaze, he watched the motion, the erotic penetration of two bodies becoming one.

Unable to stop the flow, the rise of his orgasm, he pushed deeper still. She moved with him, milking his body, intensifying the dance.

And when she chanted his name, whispering sweetly in his ear, he lost the battle and gave her his seed, the warm, pulsing fluid they both hoped would create a child.

Spent, he rested his forehead against hers. She made a soft sighing sound, and he thought about how incredible it was to be married.

"I love you," she said, her voice filled with emotion.

He smiled at her, his beautiful, perfect wife. "Me, too."

"So you're not nervous anymore?" she asked.

"No. I can face anything, Jenny. As long as you're beside me."

They finished getting dressed, and he admired the long, slim line of her gown. The white fabric, adorned with sequins, caught the light, twinkling like a thousand wish-inspired stars.

A short time later they arrived at the country club ballroom. A row of windows offered a third-story view of the garden, and a covered portico served as a balcony, rich with potted plants and intimate seating. The room itself was lush and grand, with a vaulted ceiling and chandeliers casting crystal-enhanced light.

The cocktail hour, Hawk noticed, was in full swing. Men in tuxedos and women dripping with jewels mingled freely.

He spotted his father among the crowd. Kate stood at his side, looking graceful and elegant in an emerald-colored gown.

"They're dating again," Jenny said. "Trying to mend their relationship."

"I'm glad," he responded. He was too happy to be bitter, to happy to wish ill upon others.

Hawk and Jenny crossed the room, and as they reached the balcony, they stopped to smile at each other, lured by the moonlight, the mist, the moment of contentment.

"We're magic," she said.

"Yes," he agreed, knowing that somewhere in the sky, a hawk and a dove soared through the night, their wings fanning in perfect harmony.

Ready to embrace his family, to take his place in society, Hawk slipped his arm around his wife, the woman, the delicate angel, who had healed the lone wolf's heart.

*   *   *   *   *

Don't miss the next story from
Silhouette's
LONE STAR COUNTRY CLUB:
THE MARRIAGE PROFILE
by Metsy Hingle

Available April 2003

Turn the page for an excerpt from this
exciting romance!

One

"They aren't going to show."

Ignoring his deputy's remark, Sheriff Justin Wainwright kept his eyes trained on the entrance of the Mission Creek Memorial Hospital and watched as one by one the movers and shakers of Lone Star County, Texas, strolled indoors. It seemed no one wanted to miss the dedication ceremony of the hospital's new state-of-the-art maternity ward, Justin mused as he noted members of his own family and an equal number of the Carsons file through the doors.

"We're wasting our time here, Sheriff. Mercado and Del Brio aren't going to show for this shindig."

Justin cut a glance to Bobby Hunter, the strapping young man he'd hired as his deputy less than two months earlier. "They'll show," Justin assured his impatient deputy.

"You sound pretty sure about that, Sheriff."

"I am sure," Justin said.

"Don't see why." Bobby plucked a chicken wing from a passing tray and all but inhaled the thing. "From what I hear, Mercado and Del Brio aren't exactly what you'd call civic-minded members of the community."

"You heard right. They're not." Far from it, Justin thought as he declined a glass of wine with a shake of his head and continued to survey the guests' arrivals.

"So what makes you think they'll come to this dedication shindig?"

"Because neither of them will be able to stay away."

Bobby scratched his head. "Come again?"

"The whole purpose of tonight is to acknowledge Carmine Mercado for his generous bequest to the hospital in his will. Ricky will come out of respect for his late uncle and for the Mercado family name."

"And Del Brio?"

Justin smiled as he thought of the beady-eyed thug with the vicious temper. "Del Brio will come because he's paranoid. He may have beat out Ricky as Carmine's successor, but he doesn't trust Ricky. So he'll show up here tonight and flex his muscles just to make sure that Ricky and anyone else who thinks that a Mercado should be running the family business thinks twice before challenging him. He wants everyone in the family to see that he's the boss now and that he isn't going to tolerate any disloyalty."

"Well, if they're going to show, I for one wish they'd do it soon. I haven't eaten dinner yet."

"There's plenty of food here." Justin gestured at the half-dozen tiny sandwiches and finger foods the deputy had piled on his plate. He didn't bother pointing out that the younger man had already consumed enough food to feed several people.

Bobby looked down at his plate. "I need something that will stick to my ribs."

"So, cowboy, when we're finished here, you might want to try Coyote Harry's or the Mission Creek Café. There's no charge for seconds on the specials."

"Yeah, but the food at the club's better."

Justin cocked his brow at his deputy. "You sure it's the food here you're interested in? What about that little blond waitress I saw you talking to?"

For the space of a heartbeat Justin could have sworn he saw a flicker of alarm in the other man's eyes. Then Bobby scratched his head and gave him a perplexed look. "The one with those sexy dimples?"

"No. That's Marilee, and she's a brunette," Justin said.

Bobby shrugged. His lips spread into what Justin considered a college-boy grin. "She's a real looker."

"She's also married—to a fellow who rides bulls for a living. You might want to steer clear of that one."

Bobby grinned. "Whatever you say."

Justin nodded, took a sip of the plain soda he'd been nursing since his arrival before discarding it on the tray of a passing waiter. "I'm going to move around a bit, see if I can pick up on anything. You might want to do the same."

"Will do," Bobby told him. "Want me to start over there where Johnny Mercado's holding court?"

Justin followed the direction of his deputy's gaze, frowned as he noted that Bobby was right. Surrounded by several members of the crime family and speaking emphatically about something, Johnny did seem to be holding court—which didn't fit with the older man's normally fade-into-the-background demeanor. Justin had concluded long ago that Johnny Mercado hadn't been cut out for the business of crime he'd been born into. He was too weak-willed and lacked the ruthlessness of his late brother, Carmine.

Unfortunately that criminal gene hadn't bypassed Johnny's son, Ricky.

"Looks like you were right," Bobby told him. "Del Brio just walked in."

Shifting his attention to the doorway, Justin tracked Frank Del Brio as he strutted into the reception flanked by two of his henchmen. He made his way over to where Johnny and his cohorts had gathered.

"Want me to see if I can get closer and find out what they're talking about?" Bobby asked.

"Not yet," Justin said, noting the adversarial body language between the two men. "Let's see what happens first."

Del Brio leaned in, said something to Johnny. Nearly a half a foot taller and a lot leaner than Johnny, Del Brio blocked the older man's face momentarily. But when Del Brio straightened, Justin caught a brief glimpse of Johnny's furious expression—just before Johnny lunged at Del Brio. "Aw, hell," Justin muttered, and started to move in before things got ugly.

At the sight of Johnny's pals restraining him, Justin halted in midstride. "Hang on a second," he told Bobby, who nearly collided with his back. Still poised to step in if necessary, he waited and watched as a smug-looking Del Brio sauntered off, leaving an angry Johnny Mercado staring after him.

Bobby nodded. "Wonder what Del Brio said to set Mercado off."

"Yeah. I think I'll go have a little chat with Johnny and see if I can find out. In the meantime, keep your eye on Del Brio."

"Will do. I—" Bobby's jaw dropped. He let out a

low whistle. "Man, how come these wise guys have all the luck when it comes to women?"

At his deputy's comment, Justin turned to see what had put that dumbstruck look on Bobby's face.

And his own jaw dropped at the sight of Angela.

Feeling as though he'd been sucker-punched, Justin needed a moment to regain his breath as he watched her greet one of the hospital's board members. Emotions stormed through him at breakneck speed—anger, disbelief, regret. He stared at her, noted that her hair was shorter now than it had been five years ago, a cap of sexy dark curls that framed her face and emphasized her cheekbones and those incredible blue eyes. She was thinner, too, he decided, as he followed the lines of the little black dress that skimmed her breasts, her waist, the curve of her hips. Disgusted by the unmistakable tug of sexual awareness, Justin scrubbed a hand down his face.

Get a grip, Wainwright.

"Sheriff, you all right?"

"I'm fine," Justin ground out as he struggled to regain control of himself.

"So I take it you know the lady?"

"Yeah, I know her."

"All right, so how well do you know her?"

"I guess I know Angela about as well as any man can claim to know his ex-wife."

Where Texas society reigns supreme—and appearances are *everything!*

Collect three (3) original proofs of purchase from the back pages of three (3) Lone Star Country Club titles and receive a free Lone Star book (regularly retailing at $4.75 U.S./$5.75 CAN.) that's not yet available in retail outlets!

Just complete the order form and send it, along with three (3) proofs of purchase from three (3) different Lone Star titles to: Lone Star Country Club, P.O. Box 9047, Buffalo, NY 14269-9047, or P.O. Box 613, Fort Erie, Ontario L2A 5X3.

----

093 KJH DNC3

Name (PLEASE PRINT)

Address   Apt. #

City   State/Prov.   Zip/Postal Code

Please specify which title(s) you would like to receive:

- ❑   0-373-61364-4   *Her Sweet Talkin' Man*
- ❑   0-373-61365-2   *Mission Creek Mother-To-Be*
- ❑   0-373-61366-0   *The Lawman*
- ❑   0-373-61367-9   *Doctor Seduction*

❑   Have you enclosed your proofs of purchase?

Remember—for each title selected, you must send three (3) original proofs of purchase. To receive all four (4) titles, just send in twelve (12) proofs of purchase, one from each of the 12 Lone Star Country Club titles.

One Proof of Purchase LSCCPOP10

Visit us at www.lonestarcountryclub.com   LSCCPOP10

eHARLEQUIN.com

Sit back, relax and enhance your romance
with our great magazine reading!

- **Sex and Romance!** Like your romance
  hot? Then you'll *love* the sensual reading
  in this area.

- **Quizzes!** Curious about your lovestyle?
  His commitment to you? Get the
  answers here!

- **Romantic Guides and Features!**
  Unravel the mysteries of love with
  informative articles and advice!

- **Fun Games!** Play to your heart's content....

**Plus...romantic recipes,
top ten lists,
Lovescopes...and more!**

**Enjoy our online magazine today—
visit www.eHarlequin.com!**

LONE STAR LSCC COUNTRY CLUB EST. 1923

If you missed the first exciting stories from the Lone Star Country Club, here's a chance to order your copies today!

0-373-61352-0	STROKE OF FORTUNE by Christine Rimmer	___ $4.75 U.S.	___ $5.75 CAN.
0-373-61353-9	TEXAS ROSE by Marie Ferrarella	___ $4.75 U.S.	___ $5.75 CAN.
0-373-61354-7	THE REBEL'S RETURN by Beverly Barton	___ $4.75 U.S.	___ $5.75 CAN.
0-373-61355-5	HEARTBREAKER by Laurie Paige	___ $4.75 U.S.	___ $5.75 CAN.
0-373-61356-3	PROMISED TO A SHEIK by Carla Cassidy	___ $4.75 U.S.	___ $5.75 CAN.
0-373-61357-1	THE QUIET SEDUCTION by Dixie Browning	___ $4.75 U.S.	___ $5.75 CAN.
0-373-61358-X	AN ARRANGED MARRIAGE by Peggy Moreland	___ $4.75 U.S.	___ $5.75 CAN.
0-373-61359-8	THE MERCENARY by Allison Leigh	___ $4.75 U.S.	___ $5.75 CAN.
0-373-61360-1	THE LAST BACHELOR by Judy Christenberry	___ $4.75 U.S.	___ $5.75 CAN.

(Limited quantities available.)

TOTAL AMOUNT $_____

POSTAGE & HANDLING $_____

($1.00 for one book, 50¢ for each additional)

APPLICABLE TAXES* $_____

<u>TOTAL PAYABLE</u> $_____

(Check or money order—please do not send cash)

To order, send the completed form along with your name, address, zip or postal code, along with a check or money order for the total above, payable to **Lone Star Country Club,** to:

In the U.S.: 3010 Walden Avenue, P.O. Box 9047, Buffalo, NY 14269-9047; **In Canada:** P.O. Box 616, Fort Erie, Ontario L2A 5X3

Name:_____

Address:_____ City:_____

State/Prov:_____ Zip/Postal Code:_____

Account Number (if applicable):_____

093 KJH DNC 3

  *New York residents remit applicable sales taxes.

  *Canadian residents remit applicable GST and provincial taxes.

Visit us at www.lonestarcountryclub.com   LSCCBACK-9

Coming in April 2003

baby and all

Three brand-new stories about the trials and triumphs of motherhood.

"Somebody Else's Baby"
by *USA TODAY* bestselling author Candace Camp

Widow Cassie Weeks had turned away from the world—until her stepdaughter's baby turned up on her doorstep. This tiny new life— and her gorgeous new neighbor—would teach Cassie she had a lot more living…and loving to do….

"The Baby Bombshell" by Victoria Pade

Robin Maguire knew nothing about babies or romance. But lucky for her, when she suddenly inherited an infant, the sexy single father across the hall was more than happy to teach her about both.

"Lights, Camera…Baby!" by Myrna Mackenzie

When Eve Carpenter and her sexy boss were entrusted with caring for their CEO's toddler, the formerly baby-wary executive found herself wanting to be a real-life mother—and her boss's real-life wife.

Silhouette®
TM

Where love comes alive™